FAERIES SPRITES & MALEVOLENT SPIRITS

First published in Great Britain in 2025 by Pyramid, an imprint of
Octopus Publishing Group Ltd
Carmelite House
50 Victoria Embankment
London EC4Y 0DZ
www.octopusbooks.co.uk

An Hachette UK Company
www.hachette.co.uk

The authorized representative in the EEA is Hachette Ireland,
8 Castlecourt Centre, Dublin 15, D15 XTP3, Ireland (email: info@hbgi.ie)

Text copyright © Octopus Publishing Group Ltd 2025

Distributed in the US by Hachette Book Group
1290 Avenue of the Americas, 4th and 5th Floors
New York, NY 10104

Distributed in Canada by Canadian Manda Group
664 Annette St., Toronto, Ontario, Canada M6S 2C8

All rights reserved. No part of this work may be reproduced or utilized in any form or by any means, electronic or mechanical, including photocopying, recording or by any information storage and retrieval system, without the prior written permission of the publisher.

ISBN 978-0-7537-3564-0

A CIP catalogue record for this book is available from the British Library.

Printed and bound in Great Britain.

10 9 8 7 6 5 4 3 2 1

Publisher: Lucy Pessell
Designer: Isobel Platt
Senior Editor: Tim Leng
Assistant Editor: Samina Rahman

Picture Credits: iStock/Extezty, ggodby

This FSC® label means that materials used for the product have been responsibly sourced.

FAERIES SPRITES & MALEVOLENT SPIRITS

AN ANTHOLOGY
OF CLASSIC
POETRY & STORIES

AURORA THORNE

CONTENTS

Introduction   6

LAND OF THE FAERIE

The Fairies on the Gump • Mabel Quiller-Couch	9
Water-Lilies. A Fairy Song • Felicia Hemans	18
The Fairies' Ball • Ilsien Nathalie Gaylord	19
Fairy-Land • Edgar Allan Poe	22
The Fairy Pendant • W B Yeats	24
Gramarye • Madison Julius Cawein	26
Faerie • Emma Lazarus	28
from *Phantastes* • George Macdonald	29
The Fairy's Gift • Andrew Lang	31
Fairies in the Malverns • Rose Fyleman	32
The Faery Forest • Sara Teasdale	34
from *Daniel Deronda* • George Eliot	35

THE FAE FOLK

The Lore of Proserpine • Maurice Hewlett	37
from *A Midsummer Night's Dream* • William Shakespeare	42
The Lepracaun or Fairy Shoemaker • William Allingham	43
Overheard on a Saltmarsh • Harold Monro	46
The Queen of Fairy Land • Rudyard Kipling	47
The Sea-Fairies • Alfred Lord Tennyson	48
The Faery Chasm • William Wordsworth	50
from *Nymphidia* • Michael Drayton	51
Faun • Robert Graves	54
Fairy Revels • Anne Hunter	55
Moon Fairies • Madison Julius Cawein	56
Robin Goodfellow • Unknown	59
The Wee Folk • Donald Mackenzie	60
from *The Culprit Fay* • Joseph Rodman Drake	62
The Brownies' Feast • Palmer Cox	63
Songs of the Pixies • Samuel Taylor Coleridge	67
Näcken • Erik Johan Stagnelius	71

SEDUCTION, LOVE SPELLS & CHARMS

The Rose-Elf • Hans Christian Andersen	73
The Song of Wandering Aengus • W B Yeats	79
La Belle Dame Sans Merci • John Keats	80
Thrice Toss These Oaken Ashes • Thomas Campion	82
from *Tristram and Iseult* • Matthew Arnold	83
The Fairy Well of Lagnanay • Samuel Ferguson	85
The Ballad of the Fairy Thorn-Tree • Dora Sigerson Shorter	88
from *Ballad of Tam Lin* • Robert Burns	90
My Fairy Lover • Donald A Mackenzie	92
The Ballad of Sir Olof in the Elve-Dance • Thomas Keightley	94

MISCHIEF & MALEVOLENCE

from *The Fairy Fleet* • George Macdonald	97
The Changeling by Charlotte Mew	103
The Erl-King • Johann Wolfgang von Goethe	106
Fairy Tale • James McIntyre	108
Where They Come Unto the Faery's Court • John Keats	110
The Fairies' Dance • Thomas Ravenscroft	113
The Fairies • William Allingham	114
The Stolen Child • W B Yeats	116
The Fairy Thorn • Samuel Ferguson	118
The Changeling • Donald Mackenzie	121
The Fairy • William Blake	122
Tam O' Shanter • Robert Burns	123
The Mocking Fairy • Walter de la Mare	130
The Naughty Fay • Oliver Herford	131
The Fairy Child • John Anster	132
Down-Adown-Derry by Walter de la Mare	134
The Fairies' Passage • James Clarence Mangan	137
The Fairy Changeling • Dora Sigerson Shorter	140
The Fairy Tempter • Samuel Lover	142
from *A Midsummer Night's Dream* • William Shakespeare	143

INTRODUCTION

The literary world has long been enchanted by fairies — captivating, mystical beings who weave a delicate thread between the natural and supernatural worlds. Often characterized as having otherworldly beauty, mischievous tendencies, and tied to the natural world, these diminutive, ethereal beings have evolved over cultures and centuries, reflecting perceptions of the magical and mysteries of the unknown.

The fairies of ancient folklore, particularly in Irish and Scottish tales, were often portrayed as powerful, mysterious entities closely connected to nature. With deep roots in pagan traditions, the *Sidhe* (Fae) were believed to inhabit an unseen space, one that existed at the edge of human perception. In early representations, these fairies were both benevolent guardians and malevolent tricksters, and their duality echoed a sense of awe and fear for the untamed natural world, a theme that remained as they moved from the oral tradition to written.

During the Renaissance, fairies were depicted in a radically different manner, as seen in William Shakespeare's works. Throughout *A Midsummer Night's Dream*, you'll find fairies such as Oberon, Titania, and Puck embodying both enchanting and chaotic elements. Although still powerful, Shakespeare's fairies (and goblins) became more playful and anthropomorphic, eschewing the folkloric elements of earlier depictions.

It was during the Romantic period that fairies were further transformed, being associated with the sublime and the poetic imagination. The romantic poets of the 19th century, such as John Keats, infused fairies with ethereal melancholy and sensuality in works like "Lamia" and "La Belle Dame sans Merci". These creatures became metaphors for beauty, transience and the fragility of all-too-human desires. During the Victorian era, fairies were seen as symbols of innocence and escapism while also serving as mediators between earthly and divine realms due to the period's fascination with spiritualism and the occult.

Throughout literature, fairies have served as mirrors of human imagination, reflecting our fears, desires and hopes while enchanting us with their allure. This volume of poetry and prose celebrates these complex, ethereal creatures, ranging from the whimsical and lyrical to the deeply disturbing and hypnotic.

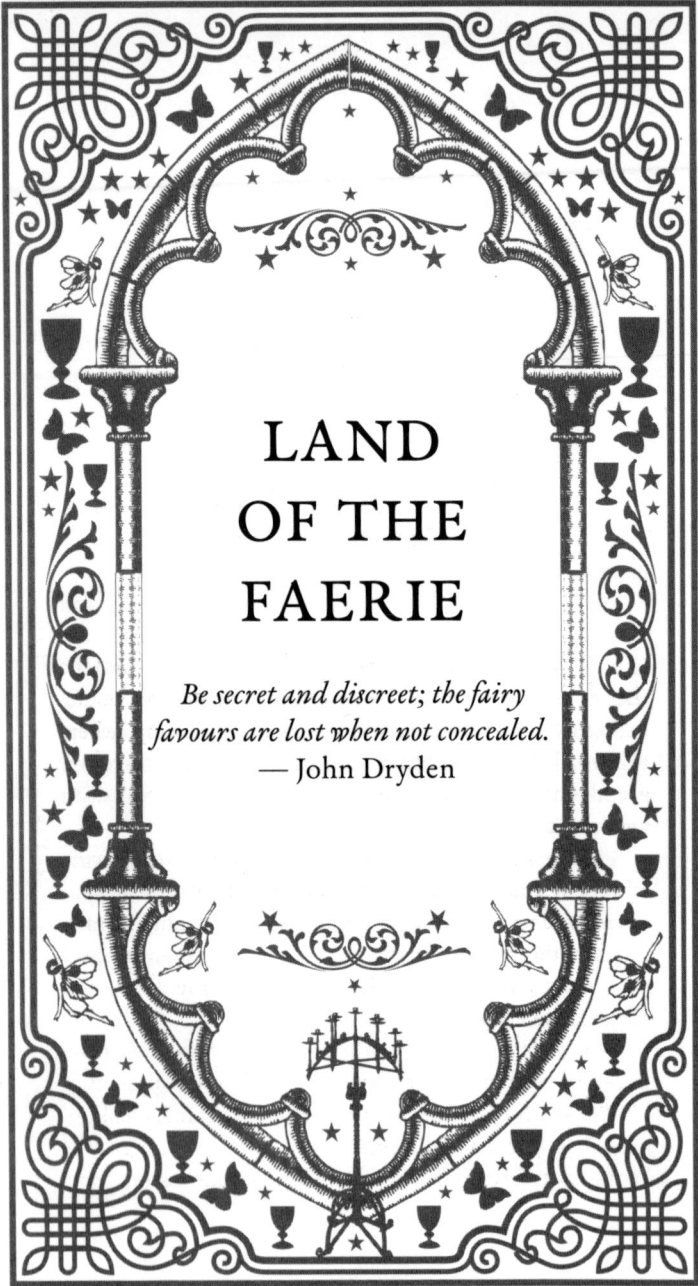

LAND OF THE FAERIE

Be secret and discreet; the fairy favours are lost when not concealed.
— John Dryden

THE FAIRIES ON THE GUMP

MABEL QUILLER-COUCH

Down by St. Just, not far from Cape Cornwall and the sea, is a small hill, — or a very large mound would, perhaps, be the truer description, — called 'The Gump,' where the Small People used to hold their revels, and where our grandfathers and grandmothers used to be allowed to stand and look on and listen.

In those good old times fairies and ordinary people were all good friends together, and it is because they were all such friends and trusted one another so, that our grandfathers and grandmothers were able to tell their grandchildren so many tales about fairies, and piskies, and buccas, and all the rest of the Little People.

People believed in the Fairies in those days, so the Fairies in return often helped the people, and did them all sorts of kindnesses. Indeed, they would do so now if folks had not grown so learned and disbelieving. It seems strange that because they have got more knowledge of some matters, they should have grown more ignorant of others, and declare that there never were such things as Fairies, just because they have neither the eyes nor the minds to see them!

Of course, no one could expect the sensitive little creatures to appear when they are sneered at and scoffed at. All the same, though, they are as much about us as ever they were, and if you or I, who do believe in the Little People, were to go to the Gump on the right nights at the right hour, we should see them feasting and dancing and holding their revels just as of old. If, though, you do go, you must be very careful to keep at a distance, and not to trespass on their fairy ground, for that is a great offence, and woe be to you if you offend them!

There was, once upon a time, a grasping, mean old fellow who did so, and pretty well he was punished for his daring. It is his story I am going to tell you, but I will not tell you his name, for that would be unpleasant for his descendants, but I will tell you this much, — he was a St. Just man, and no credit to the place either, I am sure.

Well, this old man used to listen to the tales the people told of the Fairies and their riches, and their wonderful treasures, until he could scarcely bear to hear any more, he longed so to have some of those riches for himself; and at last his covetousness grew so great, he said to himself he must and would have some, or he should die of vexation.

So one night, when the Harvest Moon was at the full, he started off alone, and very stealthily, to walk to the Gump, for he did not want his neighbours to know anything at all about his plans. He was very nervous, for it is a very desolate spot, but his greed was greater than his fear, and he made himself go forward, though he longed all the time to turn tail and hurry home to the safe shelter of his house and his bed.

When he was still at some distance from the enchanted spot, strains of the most exquisite music anyone could possibly imagine reached his ear, and as he stood listening it seemed to come nearer and nearer until, at last, it was close about him.

The most wonderful part, though, of it all was that there was nothing to be seen, no person, no bird, not an animal even. The empty moor stretched away on every side, the Gump lay bare and desolate before him. The only living being on it that night was himself.

The music, indeed, seemed to come from under the ground, and such strange music it was, too, so gentle, so touching, it made the old miser weep, in spite of himself, and then, even while the tears were still running down his cheeks, he was forced to laugh quite merrily, and even to dance, though he certainly did not want to do either. After that it was not surprising that he found himself marching along, step and step, keeping time with the music as it played, first slowly and with stately tread, then fast and lively.

All the time, though, that he was laughing and weeping, marching or dancing, his wicked mind was full of thoughts as to how he should get at the fairy treasure.

At last, when he got close to the Gump, the music ceased, and suddenly, with a loud crashing noise which nearly scared the old man out of his senses, the whole hill seemed to open as if by magic, and in one instant every spot was lighted up. Thousands of little lights of all colours gleamed everywhere, silver stars twinkled and sparkled on every furze-bush, tiny lamps hung from every blade of grass. It was a more lovely sight than one ever sees nowadays, more lovely than any pantomime one has ever seen or ever will see. Then, out from the open hill marched troops of little Spriggans.

Spriggans, you must know, are the Small People who live in rocks and stones, and cromlechs, the most mischievous, thievish little creatures that ever lived, and woe betide anyone who meddles with their dwelling-places.

Well, first came all those Spriggans, then a large band of musicians followed by troops of soldiers, each troop carrying a beautiful banner, which waved and streamed out as though a brisk breeze were blowing, whereas in reality there was not a breath of wind stirring. These hosts of Little People quickly took up their places in perfect order all about the Gump, and, though they appeared quite unconscious of his presence, a great number formed a ring all round the old man. He was greatly amazed, but, "Never mind," he thought, "they are such little whipper-snappers I can easily squash them with my foot if they try on any May-games with me."

As soon as the musicians, the Spriggans, and the soldiers had arranged themselves, out came a lot of servants carrying most lovely gold and silver vessels, goblets, too, cut out of single rubies, and diamonds, and emeralds, and every kind of precious stone. Then came others bearing rich meats and pastry, luscious fruits and preserves, everything, in fact, that one could think of that was dainty and appetizing. Each servant placed his burden on the tables in its proper place, then silently retired.

Can you not imagine how the glorious scene dazzled the old man, and how his eyes glistened, and his fingers itched to grab at some of the wonderful things and carry them off? He knew that even one only of those flashing goblets would make him rich for ever.

He was just thinking that nowhere in the world could there be a more beautiful sight, when, lo and behold! the illumination became twenty times as brilliant, and out of the hill came thousands and thousands of exquisitely dressed ladies and gentlemen, all in rows, each gentleman leading a lady, and all marching in perfect time and order.

They came in companies of a thousand each, and each company was differently attired. In the first the gentlemen were all dressed in yellow satin covered with copper-coloured spangles, on their heads they wore copper-coloured helmets with waving, yellow plumes, and on their feet yellow shoes with copper heels. The flashing of the copper in the moonlight was almost blinding. Their companions all were dressed alike in white satin gowns edged with large turquoises, and on their tiny feet pale blue shoes with buckles formed of one large turquoise set in pearls.

The gentlemen conducted the ladies to their places on the Gump, and with a courtly bow left them, themselves retiring to a little distance. The next troop then came up, in this the gentlemen were all attired in black, trimmed with silver, silver helmets with black plumes, black stockings and silver shoes. Their ladies were dressed in pink embroidered in gold, with waving pink plumes in their hair, and golden buckles on their pink shoes. In the next troop the men were dressed in blue and white, the ladies in green, with diamonds all around the hem of the gown, diamonds flashing in their hair, and hanging in long ropes from their necks; on their green shoes single diamonds blazed and flashed.

So they came, troop after troop, more than I can describe, or you could remember, only I must tell you that the last of all were the most lovely. The ladies, all of whom had dark hair, were clad in white velvet lined with the palest violet silk, while round the hems of the skirts and on the bodices were bands of soft white swansdown. Swansdown also edged the little violet cloaks which hung from their shoulders. I cannot describe to you how beautiful they looked, with their rosy, smiling faces, and long black curls. On their heads they wore little silver crowns set with amethysts, amethysts, too, sparkled on their necks and over their gowns. In their hands they carried long trails of the lovely blossom of the wistaria. Their companions were clad in white and green, and in their left hands they carried silver rods with emerald stars at the top.

It really seemed at one time as though the troops of Little People would never cease pouring out of the hill. They did so at last, though, and as soon as all were in their places the music suddenly changed, and became more exquisite than ever.

The old man by this time seemed able to see more clearly, and hear more distinctly, and his sense of smell grew keener. Never were such flashing gems as here, never had any flowers such scents as these that were here.

There were now thousands of little ladies gathered on the Gump, and these all broke out into song at the same instant, such beautiful singing, too, so sweet and delicate. The words were in an unknown tongue, but the song was evidently about some great personages who were about to emerge from the amazing hill, for again it opened, and again poured forth a crowd of Small People.

First of all came a bevy of little girls in white gauze, scattering flowers, which, as soon as they touched the ground, sprang up into full life and threw out leaves and more flowers, full of exquisite scents; then came a number of boys playing on shells as though they were harps, and making ravishing music, while after them came hundreds and hundreds of little men clad in green and gold, followed by a perfect forest of banners spreading and waving on the air.

Then last, but more beautiful than all that had gone before, was carried a raised platform covered with silk embroidered with real gold, and edged with crystals, and on the platform were seated a prince and princess of such surpassing loveliness that no words can be found to describe them. They were dressed in the richest velvet, and covered with precious stones which blazed and sparkled in the myriad lights until the eye could scarce bear to look at them.

Over her lovely robe the princess's hair flowed down to the floor, where it rested in great shining, golden waves. In her hand she held a golden sceptre, on the top of which blazed a diamond as large as a walnut, while the prince carried one with a sapphire of equal size. After a deal of marching backwards and forwards, the platform was placed on the highest point of the Gump, which was now a hill of flowers, and every fairy walked up and bowed, said something to the prince and princess, and passed on to a seat at the tables. And the marvel was that though there were so many fairies present, there was not the slightest confusion amongst them, not one person moved out of place at the wrong moment. All was as quiet and well-arranged as could possibly be.

At length all were seated, whereupon the prince gave a signal, on which a number of footmen came forward carrying a table laden with dainty food in solid gold dishes, and wines in goblets of precious stones which they placed on the platform before the prince and princess. As soon as the royal pair began to eat, all the hosts around them followed their example, and such a merry, jovial meal they had. The viands disappeared as fast as they could go, laughter and talk sounded on all sides, and never a sign did any of them give that they knew that a human being was watching them. If they knew it, they showed not the slightest concern.

"Ah!" thought the old miser to himself. "I can't get all I'd like to, but if I could reach up to the prince's table I could get enough at one grab to set me up for life, and make me the richest man in St. Just parish!"

Stooping down, he slowly and stealthily dragged himself nearer and nearer to the table. He felt quite sure that no one could see him. What he himself did not see was that hundreds of wicked little Spriggans had tied ropes on to him, and were holding fast to the ends. He crawled and crawled so slowly and carefully that it took him some time to get over the ground, but he managed it at last, and got quite close up to the lovely little pair. Once there he paused for a moment and looked back, — perhaps to see if the way was clear for him to run when he had done what he meant to do. He was rather startled to find that all was as dark as dark could be, and that he could see nothing at all behind him. However, he tried to cheer himself by thinking that it was only that his eyes were dazzled by looking at the bright lights so long. He was even more startled, though, when he turned round to the Gump again, to find that every eye of all those hundreds and thousands of fairies on the hill was looking straight into his eyes. At first he was really frightened, but as they did nothing but look, he told himself that they could not really be gazing at him, and grew braver with the thought. Then slowly bringing up his hat, as a boy does to catch a butterfly, he was just going to bring it down on the silken platform and capture prince and princess, table, gold dishes and all, when hark! A shrill whistle sounded, the old man's hand, with the hat in it, was paralysed in the air, so that he could not move it backwards or forwards, and in an instant every light went out, and all was pitchy darkness.

There were a whir-r-r and a buzz, and a whir-r-r, as if a swarm of bees were flying by him, and the old man felt himself fastened so securely to the ground that, do what he would, he could not move an inch, and all the time he felt himself being pinched, and pricked, and tweaked from top to toe, so that not an inch of him was free from torment. He was lying on his back at the foot of the Gump, though how he got there he could never tell. His arms were stretched out and fastened down, so that he could not do anything to drive off his tormentors, his legs were so secured that he could not even relieve himself by kicking, and his tongue was tied with cords, so that he could not call out.

There he lay, no one knows how long, for to him it seemed hours, and no one else but the fairies knew anything about it. At last he felt a lot of little feet running over him, but whose they were he had no idea until something perched on his nose, and by the light of the moon he saw it was a Spriggan. His wicked old heart sank when he realized that he had got into their clutches, for all his life he had heard what wicked little creatures they were.

The little imp on his nose kicked and danced and stamped about in great delight at finding himself perched up so high. We all know how painful it is to have one's nose knocked, even ever so little, so you may imagine that the old miser did not enjoy himself at all. Master Spriggan did, though. He roared with laughter, as though he were having a huge joke, until at last, rising suddenly to his feet and standing on the tips of his tiny toes, he shouted sharply, "Away! away! I smell the day!" and to the old man's great relief off he flew in a great hurry, followed by all his mischievous little companions who had been playing games, and running races all over their victim's body.

Left at last to himself, the mortified old man lay for some time, thinking over all that had happened, trying to collect his senses, and wondering how he should manage to escape from his bonds, for he might lie there for a week without any human being coming near the place.

Till sunrise he lay there, trying to think of some plan, and then, what do you think he saw? Why, that he had not been tied down by ropes at all, but only by thousands of gossamer webs! And there they were now, all over him, with the dew on them sparkling like the diamonds that the princess had worn the night before. And those dewdrop diamonds were all the jewels he got for his night's work.

When he made this discovery he turned over and groaned and wept with rage and shame, and never, to his dying day, could he bear to look at sparkling gold or gems, for the mere sight of them made him feel quite ill.

At last, afraid lest he should be missed, and searchers be sent out to look for him, he got up, brushed off the dewy webs, and putting on his battered old hat, crept slowly home. He was wet through with dew, cold, full of rheumatism, and very ashamed of himself, and very good care he took to keep that night's experiences to himself. No one must know his shame.

Years after, though, when he had become a changed man, and repented of his former greediness, he let out the story bit by bit to be a lesson to others, until his friends and neighbours, who loved to listen to anything about fairies, had gathered it all as I have told it to you here. And you may be quite sure it is all true, for the old man was not clever enough to invent it.

WATER-LILIES.
A FAIRY SONG

FELICIA HEMANS

Come away, elves! — while the dew is sweet,
Come to the dingles where fairies meet!
Know that the lilies have spread their bells
O'er all the pools in our forest dells;
Stilly and lightly their vases rest
On the quivering sleep of the water's breast,
Catching the sunshine through leaves that throw
To their scented bosoms an emerald glow;
And a star from the depth of each pearly cup,
A golden star unto heaven looks up,
As if seeking its kindred where bright they lie,
Set in the blue of the summer sky.
Come away! Under arching boughs we'll float,
Making those urns each a fairy boat;
We'll row them with reeds o'er the fountains free,
And a tall flag-leaf shall our streamer be;
And we'll send out wild music so sweet and low,
It shall seem from the bright flower's heart to flow,
As if 'twere a breeze with a flute's low sigh,
Or water-drops train'd into melody.
Come away! for the midsummer sun grows strong,
And the life of the lily may not be long.

THE FAIRIES' BALL

ILSIEN NATHALIE GAYLORD

Listen, Dearie! What do you suppose I've just heard
    Over in the Arbor there,
Where the roses are nodding and whispering low,
    All in the soft evening air?

Why, the Fairies are coming to have a dance
    Right in our Garden, Dear!
For this is Mid-summer Night, you know,
    The Elfin time of the year.

All the Fairies are coming from everywhere,
    To dance in the moonlight here;
And they're going to dress in the loveliest things
    You ever dreamed of, Dear!

There'll be the Fairies of the Moon, of course,
    All dressed in misty white,
With beautiful silvery gauzy wings;
    And a star-tipped wand for light.

They'll skip along down the moonbeams, Dear,
    So I heard the roses say,
A lovely, dancing shimmering band,
    Twinkling all the way!

And the little Fairies of the Clouds, you know,
    They're coming, too, with the rest.
And what will you say when I tell you, Dear,
How those darling little Fairies'll be dressed?

* * *

Why, they're just going to bundle themselves all up
In lovely sunset clouds,
And come trailing along down the sky to us,
In beautiful shining crowds.

Some of the very, very littlest ones
Will dress in pinky white,
And some of the others in orange, and red,
All fringed with golden light.

And then there're the dear little Water-fairies, too,
You can't guess how sweet they'll be!
In little dresses of white foam-mist,
All hung with pearls from the sea.

And the little Queen of the Flowers'll be there,
Sitting up on her lovely throne.
Just wait till I tell you about it, Dear —
You'll wish 'twas your very own!

The darling little Fairies of the Snow made it, Dear,
All glistening frosty white;
Made it, up in their home in Cloudland there,
And they're bringing it down to-night.

It's just like a beautiful frosty cave,
All sparkling with diamonds, Dear,
And frosty lace-work, that'll glisten bright
Out in the moonlight here.

And the roses have made the softest carpet
Out of sweet rose-petals, you know;
And the pansies, cushions of purple velvet —
They all love their little Queen so!

And the Butterfly fairies will be there, too,
In their lovely velvet clothes,
With their beautiful wings of orange and black,
And yellow, and purple and rose.

And oh, there are ever so many more —
I can hardly remember them all!
Who're coming to-night — just think of it, Dear,
To dance at the Fairies' ball!

So hurry up, quick, and close your eyes,
For I heard the roses say
That to see the Fairies one must always come
Around by Dreamland way.

FAIRY-LAND

EDGAR ALLAN POE

ぴつ

Dim vales- and shadowy floods —
And cloudy-looking woods,
Whose forms we can't discover
For the tears that drip all over!
Huge moons there wax and wane —
Again- again- again —
Every moment of the night —
Forever changing places —
And they put out the star-light
With the breath from their pale faces.
About twelve by the moon-dial,
One more filmy than the rest
(A kind which, upon trial,
They have found to be the best)
Comes down- still down- and down,
With its centre on the crown
Of a mountain's eminence,
While its wide circumference
In easy drapery falls
Over hamlets, over halls,
Wherever they may be-
O'er the strange woods- o'er the sea —
Over spirits on the wing —
Over every drowsy thing —
And buries them up quite
In a labyrinth of light —

And then, how deep!- O, deep!
Is the passion of their sleep.
In the morning they arise,
And their moony covering
Is soaring in the skies,
With the tempests as they toss,
Like- almost anything —
Or a yellow Albatross.
They use that moon no more
For the same end as before —
Videlicet, a tent —
Which I think extravagant:
Its atomies, however,
Into a shower dissever,
Of which those butterflies
Of Earth, who seek the skies,
And so come down again,
(Never-contented things!)
Have brought a specimen
Upon their quivering wings.

THE FAIRY PENDANT

W B YEATS

Scene: A circle of Druidic stones
First Fairy: Afar from our lawn and our levee,
O sister of sorrowful gaze!
Where the roses in scarlet are heavy
And dream of the end of their days,
You move in another dominion
And hang o'er the historied stone:
Unpruned in your beautiful pinion
Who wander and whisper alone.

All: Come away while the moon's in the woodland,
We'll dance and then feast in a dairy.
Though youngest of all in our good band,
You are wasting away, little fairy.

Second Fairy: Ah! cruel ones, leave me alone now
While I murmur a little and ponder
The history here in the stone now;
Then away and away I will wander,
And measure the minds of the flowers,
And gaze on the meadow-mice wary,
And number their days and their hours —

All: You're wasting away, little fairy.

Second Fairy: O shining ones, lightly with song pass,
Ah! leave me, I pray you and beg.
My mother drew forth from the long grass
A piece of a nightingale's egg,
And cradled me here where are sung,
Of birds even, longings for aery
Wild wisdoms of spirit and tongue.

All: You're wasting away, little fairy.

First Fairy [turning away]: Though the tenderest roses
were round you,
The soul of this pitiless place
With pitiless magic has bound you —
Ah! woe for the loss of your face,
And the loss of your laugh with its lightness —
Ah! woe for your wings and your head —
Ah! woe for your eyes and their brightness —
Ah! woe for your slippers of red.

We'll dance and then feast in a dairy.
Though youngest of all in our good band,
She's wasting away, little fairy.

GRAMARYE

MADISON JULIUS CAWEIN

൶

There are some things that entertain me more
Than men or books; and to my knowledge seem
A key of Poetry, made of magic lore
Of childhood, opening many a fabled door
Of superstition, mystery, and dream
Enchantment locked of yore.

For, when through dusking woods my pathway lies,
Often I feel old spells, as o'er me flits
The bat, like some black thought that, troubled, flies
Round some dark purpose; or before me cries
The owl that, like an evil conscience, sits
A shadowy voice and eyes.

Then, when down blue canals of cloudy snow
The white moon oars her boat, and woods vibrate
With crickets, lo, I hear the hautboys blow
Of Elf-land; and when green the fireflies glow,
See where the goblins hold a Fairy Fête
With lanthorn row on row.

Strange growths, that ooze from long-dead logs and spread
A creamy fungus, where the snail, uncoiled,
And fat slug feed at morn, are Pixy bread
Made of the yeasted dew; the lichens red,
Besides these grown, are meat the Brownies broiled
Above a glow-worm bed.

The smears of silver on the webs that line
The tree's crook'd roots, or stretch, white-wove, within
The hollow stump, are stains of Faëry wine
Spilled on the cloth where Elf-land sat to dine,
When night beheld them drinking, chin to chin,
O' the moon's fermented shine.

What but their chairs the mushrooms on the lawn,
Or toadstools hidden under flower and fern,
Tagged with the dotting dew! — With knees updrawn
Far as his eyes, have I not come upon
PUCK seated there? but scarcely 'round could turn
Ere, presto! he was gone.

And so though Science from the woods hath tracked
The Elfin; and with prosy lights of day
Unhallowed all his haunts; and, dulling, blacked
Our eyesight, still hath Beauty never lacked
For seers yet; who, in some wizard way,
Prove Fancy real as Fact.

FAERIE

EMMA LAZARUS

From the oped lattice glance once more abroad
While the ethereal moontide bathes with light
Hill, stream, and garden, and white-winding road.

All gracious myths born of the shadowy night
Recur, and hover in fantastic guise,
Airy and vague, before the drowsy sight.

On yonder soft gray hill Endymion lies
In rosy slumber, and the moonlit air
Breathes kisses on his cheeks and lips and eyes.

'Twixt bush and bush gleam flower-white limbs, left bare,
Of huntress-nymphs, and flying raiment thin,
Vanishing faces, and bright floating hair.

The quaint midsummer fairies and their kin,
Gnomes, elves, and trolls, on blossom, branch, and grass
Gambol and dance, and winding out and in

Leave circles of spun dew where'er they pass.
Through the blue ether the freed Ariel flies;
Enchantment holds the air; a swarming mass

Of myriad dusky, gold-winged dreams arise,
Throng toward the gates of sense, and so possess.
The soul, and lull it to forgetfulness.

from PHANTASTES

GEORGE MACDONALD

ॐ

"Sister Snowdrop died
Before we were born."
"She came like a bride
In a snowy morn."
"What's a bride?"
"What is snow?
"Never tried."
"Do not know."

"Who told you about her?"
"Little Primrose there
Cannot do without her."
"Oh, so sweetly fair!"
"Never fear,
She will come,
Primrose dear."
"Is she dumb?"

"She'll come by-and-by."
"You will never see her."
"She went home to die,
"Till the new year."
"Snowdrop!" "'Tis no good
To invite her."
"Primrose is very rude,
"I will bite her."

* * *

"Oh, you naughty Pocket!
"Look, she drops her head."
"She deserved it, Rocket,
"And she was nearly dead."
"To your hammock — off with you!"
"And swing alone."
"No one will laugh with you."
"No, not one."

"Now let us moan."
"And cover her o'er."
"Primrose is gone."
"All but the flower."
"Here is a leaf."
"Lay her upon it."
"Follow in grief."
"Pocket has done it."

"Deeper, poor creature!
Winter may come."
"He cannot reach her —
That is a hum."
"She is buried, the beauty!"
"Now she is done."
"That was the duty."
"Now for the fun."

THE FAIRY'S GIFT

ANDREW LANG

The Fays that to my christ'ning came
(For come they did, my nurses taught me),
They did not bring me wealth or fame,
'Tis very little that they brought me.
But one, the crossest of the crew,
The ugly old one, uninvited,
Said, "I shall be avenged on you,
My child; you shall grow up short-sighted!"
With magic juices did she lave
Mine eyes, and wrought her wicked pleasure.
Well, of all gifts the Fairies gave,
Hers is the present that I treasure!

The bore whom others fear and flee,
I do not fear, I do not flee him;
I pass him calm as calm can be;
I do not cut — I do not see him!
And with my feeble eyes and dim,
Where you see patchy fields and fences,
For me the mists of Turner swim —
My "azure distance" soon commences!
Nay, as I blink about the streets
Of this befogged and miry city,
Why, almost every girl one meets
Seems preternaturally pretty!
"Try spectacles," one's friends intone;
"You'll see the world correctly through them."
But I have visions of my own,
And not for worlds would I undo them.

FAIRIES IN THE MALVERNS

ROSE FYLEMAN

As I walked over Hollybush Hill
The sun was low and the winds were still,
And never a whispering branch I heard
Nor ever the tiniest call of a bird.

And when I came to the topmost height
Oh, but I saw such a wonderful sight:
All about on the hill-crest there
The fairies danced in the golden air.

Danced and frolicked with never a sound
In and out in a magical round;
Wide and wider the circle grew
Then suddenly melted into the blue.

As I walked down into Eastnor Vale
The stars already were twinkling pale,
And over the spaces of dew-white grass
I saw a marvellous pageant pass.

Tiny riders on tiny steeds,
Decked with blossoms and armed with reeds,
With gossamer banners floating far

And a radiant queen in an ivory car.
The beeches spread their petticoats wide
And curtseyed low upon either side;
The rabbits scurried across the glade
To peep at the glittering cavalcade.

Far and farther I saw them go
And vanish into the woods below;
Then over the shadowy woodland ways
I wandered home in a sweet amaze.

But Malvern people need fear no ill
Since fairies bide in their country still.

THE FAERY FOREST

SARA TEASDALE

The faery forest glimmered
   Beneath an ivory moon,
The silver grasses shimmered
   Against a faery tune.

Beneath the silken silence
   The crystal branches slept,
And dreaming thro' the dew-fall
   The cold white blossoms wept.

from
DANIEL DERONDA

GEORGE ELIOT

Fairy folk a-listening
Hear the seed sprout in the spring,
And for music to their dance
Hear the hedgerows wake from trance,
Sap that trembles into buds
Sending little rhythmic floods
Of fairy sound in fairy ears.
Thus all beauty that appears
Has birth as sound to finer sense
And lighter-clad intelligence.

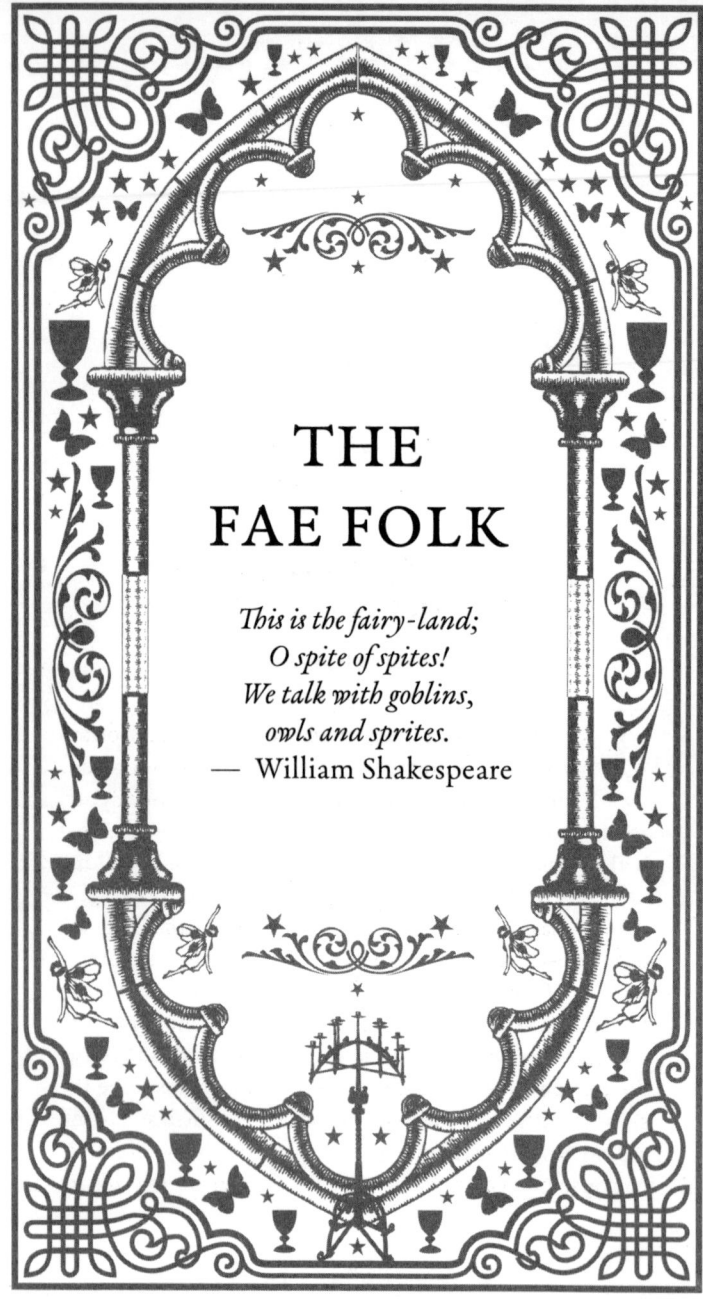

THE FAE FOLK

*This is the fairy-land;
O spite of spites!
We talk with goblins,
owls and sprites.*
— William Shakespeare

THE LORE OF PROSERPINE

MAURICE HEWLETT

There is a chain of Being of whose top alike and bottom we know nothing at all. What we do know is that our own is a link in it, and cannot generally, can only fitfully and rarely, have intercourse with any other. I am not prepared with any modern instances of intercourse with the animal and vegetable world, even to such a limited extent, for instance, as that of Balaam with his ass, or that of Achilles with his horses; but I suspect that there are an enormous number unrecorded. Speech, of course, is not necessary to such an intercourse. Speech is a vehicle of human intercourse, but not of that of any other created order so far as we know. Birds and beasts do not converse in speech, smell or touch seems to be the sense employed; and though the vehicles of smell and touch are unknown to us, in moments of high emotion we ourselves converse otherwise than by speech. Indeed, seeing that all created things possess a spirit whereby they are what they are, it does not seem necessary to suppose intercourse impossible without speech, and I myself have never had any difficulty in accepting the stories of much more vital mixed intercourse which we read of in the Greek and other mythologies. If we read, for instance, that such and such a man or woman was the offspring of a woman and the spirit of a river, or of a man and the spirit of a hill or oak-tree, it does not seem to me at all extraordinary. The story of the wife who suffered a fairy union and bore a fairy child which disappeared with her is a case in point. The fairy father was, so far as I can make out, the indwelling spirit of a rose, and the story is too painful and the detail in my possession too exact for me to put it down here. I was myself actually present, and in the house, when the child was born. I witnessed the anguish of the unfortunate husband, who is now dead. Mr. Wentz has many instances of the kind from Ireland and other Celtic countries; but fairies are by no means confined to Celtic countries, though they are more easily discerned by Celtic races.

Of this chain of Being, then, of which our order is a member, the fairy world is another and more subtle member, subtler in the right sense of the word because it is not burdened with a material envelope. Like man, like the wind, like the rose, it has spirit; but unlike any of the lower orders, of which man is one, it has no sensible wrapping unless deliberately it consents to inhabit one. This, as we know, it frequently does. I have mentioned several cases of the kind; Mrs. Ventris was one, Mabilla By-the-Wood was another. I have not personally come across any other cases where a male fairy took upon him the burden of a man than that of Quidnunc. Even there I have never been satisfied that Quidnunc became man to the extent that Mrs. Ventris did. Quidnunc, no doubt, was the father of Lady Emily's children; but were those children human? There are some grounds for thinking so, and in that case, if "the nature follows the male,"

Quidnunc must have doffed his immateriality and suffered real incarnation. If they were fairy children the case is altered. Quidnunc need not have had a body at all. Now since it is clear that the fairy world is a real order of creation, with laws of its own every whit as fixed and immutable as those of any other order known to naturalists, it is very reasonable to inquire into the nature and scope of those laws. I am not at all prepared at present to attempt anything like a digest of them. That would require a lifetime; and no small part of the task, after marshalling the evidence, would be to agree upon terms which would be intelligible to ourselves and yet not misleading. To take polity alone, are we to understand that any kind of Government resembling that of human societies obtains among them? When we talk of Queens or Kings of the Fairies, of Oberon and Titania, for example, are we using a rough translation of a real something, or are we telling the mere truth? Is there a fairy king? The King of the Wood, for instance, who was he? Is there a fairy queen? Who is Queen Mab? Who is Despoina? Who is the Lady of the Lake? Who is the "Βασίλισσα τῶν βουνῶν," or "Μεγάλη Κυρά" of whom Mr. Lawson tells us such suggestive things in his Modern Greek Folk-lore? Who is Despoina, with whom I myself have conversed, "a dread goddess, not of human speech?" The truth, I suspect, is this. There are, as we know, countless tribes, clans, or orders of fairies, just as there are nations of men. They confess the power of some greater Spirit among themselves, bow to it instantly and submit to its decrees; but they do not, so far as I can understand, acknowledge a monarchy in any sense of ours. If there is a Supreme Power over the fairy creation it is Proserpine; but hers is too remote an empire to be comparable to any of ours. Not even Cæsar, not even the Great King, could hope to rule such myriads as she. She may stand for the invisible creation no doubt, but she would never have commerce with it. No fairy hath seen her at any time; no sovereignty such as we are now discussing would be applicable to her dominion. That of Artemis, or that of Pan, is more comparable. Artemis is certainly ruler of the spirits of the air and water, of the hills and shores of the sea, and to some extent her power overlaps that of Pan who is potent in nearly all land solitudes. But really the two lord-ships can be exactly discriminated. They never conflict. The legions of Artemis are all female, though on earth men as well as women worship her; the legions of Pan are all male, though on earth he can chasten women as well as men. But Pan can do nothing against Artemis, nor she anything against him or any of his. The decree or swift deed of either is respected by the other. They are not, then, as earthly kings, leaders of their hosts to battle against their neighbours. Fairies fight and marshal themselves for war; Mr. Wentz has several cases of the kind. But Pan and Artemis have no share in these warfares. Queen Mab is one of the many names, and points to one of the many manifestations of Artemis; the Lady of the Lake is another. Both of these have died out, and in the country she is generally hinted at under the veil of "Mistress of the Wood" or "Lady of the Hill." I heard the latter from a Wiltshire shepherd; the former is used in Sussex, in the Cheviots, and in Lincolnshire, and was introduced, I believe, by the Gipsies. Titania was a name of romance, and so was Oberon, that of her husband in romance. Queen Mab has no husband, nor will she ever have.

But she is, of course, a goddess, and not a queen in our sense of the word. The fairies, who partake of her nature just so far as we partake of theirs, pray to her, invoke her, and make her offerings every day. But a vital difference between their kind and ours is that they can see her and live; and we never see the Gods until we die.

They have no other leaders, I believe, and certainly no royal houses. Faculty is free in the fairy world to its utmost limit. A fairy's power within his own order is limited only by the extent of his personal faculty, and subject only to the

Gods. There is no civil law to restrain him, and no moral law; no law at all except the law of being.

We are contemplating, then, a realm, nay, a world, where anarchy is the rule, and anarchy in the widest sense. The fairies are of a world where Right and Wrong don't obtain, where Possible and Impossible are the only finger-posts at cross-roads; for the Gods themselves give no moral sanction to desire and hold up no moral check. The fairies love and hate intensely; they crave and enjoy; they satisfy by kindness or cruelty; they serve or enslave each other; they give life or take it as their instinct, appetite or whim may be. But there is this remarkable thing to be noted, that when a thing is dead they cannot be aware of its existence. For them it is not, it is as if it had never been. Ruth, therefore, is unknown, their emotions are maimed to that serious extent that they cannot regret, cannot pity, cannot weep for sorrow. They weep through rage, but sorrow they know not. Similarly, they cannot laugh for joy. Laughing with them is an expression of pleasure, but not of joy. Here then, at least, we have the better of them. I for one would not exchange my privilege of pity or my consolation of pure sorrow for all their transcendent faculty.

from A MIDSUMMER NIGHT'S DREAM

WILLIAM SHAKESPEARE

Over hill, over dale,
Thorough bush, thorough brier,
Over park, over pale,
Thorough flood, thorough fire,
I do wander everywhere,
Swifter than the moonè's sphere;
And I serve the fairy queen,
To dew her orbs upon the green:
The cowslips tall her pensioners be;
In their gold coats spots you see;
Those be rubies, fairy favours,
In those freckles live their savours:
I must go seek some dew-drops here,
And hang a pearl in every cowslip's ear.
Farewell, thou lob of spirits. I'll be gone.
Our queen and all her elves come here anon.

THE LEPRACAUN
OR FAIRY SHOEMAKER

WILLIAM ALLINGHAM

Little Cowboy, what have you heard,
Up on the lonely rath's green mound?
Only the plaintive yellow bird
Sighing in sultry fields around,
Chary, chary, chary, chee-ee! —
Only the grasshopper and the bee? —
"Tip-tap, rip-rap,
Tick-a-tack-too!
Scarlet leather, sewn together,
This will make a shoe.
Left, right, pull it tight;
Summer days are warm;
Underground in winter,
Laughing at the storm!"
Lay your ear close to the hill.
Do you not catch the tiny clamour,
Busy click of an elfin hammer,
Voice of the Lepracaun singing shrill
As he merrily plies his trade?
He's a span
And a quarter in height.
Get him in sight, hold him tight,
And you're a made Man!

You watch your cattle the summer day,
Sup on potatoes, sleep in the hay;
How would you like to roll in your carriage,
Look for a duchess's daughter in marriage?
Seize the Shoemaker - then you may!
    "Big boots a-hunting,
    Sandals in the hall,
    White for a wedding-feast,
    Pink for a ball.
    This way, that way,
    So we make a shoe;
    Getting rich every stitch,
    Tick-tack-too!"
Nine-and-ninety treasure-crocks
This keen miser-fairy hath,
Hid in mountains, woods, and rocks,
Ruin and round-tow'r, cave and rath,
And where the cormorants build;
    From times of old
    Guarded by him;
    Each of them fill'd
    Full to the brim
    With gold!

I caught him at work one day, myself,
In the castle-ditch where foxglove grows, —
A wrinkled, wizen'd, and bearded Elf,
Spectacles stuck on his pointed nose,
Silver buckles to his hose,
Leather apron - shoe in his lap —
    "Rip-rap, tip-tap,
    Tick-tack-too!
    (A grasshopper on my cap!
    Away the moth flew!)
    Buskins for a fairy prince,

Brogues for his son, —
Pay me well, pay me well,
When the job is done!"
The rogue was mine, beyond a doubt.
I stared at him; he stared at me;
"Servant, Sir!' 'Humph!" says he,
And pull'd a snuff-box out.
He took a long pinch, look'd better pleased,
The queer little Lepracaun;
Offer'd the box with a whimsical grace, —
Pouf! he flung the dust in my face,
And while I sneezed,
Was gone!

OVERHEARD ON A SALTMARSH

HAROLD MONRO

୨୨୧

Nymph, nymph, what are your beads?
Green glass, goblin. Why do you stare at them?
Give them me.
No.
Give them me. Give them me.
No.
Then I will howl all night in the reeds,
Lie in the mud and howl for them.

Goblin, why do you love them so?

They are better than stars or water,
Better than voices of winds that sing,
Better than any man's fair daughter,
Your green glass beads on a silver ring.

Hush I stole them out of the moon.

Give me your beads. I desire them.
No.
I will howl in a deep lagoon
For your green glass beads, I love them so.
Give them me. Give them.

THE QUEEN OF FAIRY LAND

RUDYARD KIPLING

"I have a thousand men," said he,
    "To wait upon my will;
And towers nine upon the Tyne,
    And three upon the Till."

"And what care I for your men? " said she,
    "Or towers from Tyne to Till?
Sith you must go with me," said she,
    "To wait upon my will.

And you may lead a thousand men
    Nor ever draw the rein,
But before you lead the Fairy Queen
    'Twill burst your heart in twain."

He has slipped his foot from the stirrup-bar,
    The bridle from his hand,
And he is bound by hand and foot
    To the Queen of Fairy Land.

THE SEA-FAIRIES

ALFRED LORD TENNYSON

༄༅

Slow sail'd the weary mariners and saw,
Betwixt the green brink and the running foam,
Sweet faces, rounded arms, and bosoms prest
To little harps of gold; and while they mused,
Whispering to each other half in fear,
Shrill music reach'd them on the middle sea.

Whither away, whither away, whither away? fly no more.
Whither away, from the high green field, and the happy
blossoming shore?
Day and night to the billow the fountain calls;
Down shower the gambolling waterfalls
From wandering over the lea;
Out of the live-green heart of the dells
They freshen the silvery-crimson shells,
And thick with white bells the clover-hill swells
High over the full-toned sea.
O, hither, come hither and furl your sails,
Come hither to me and to me;
Hither, come hither and frolic and play;
Here it is only the mew that wails;
We will sing to you all the day.
Mariner, mariner, furl your sails,
For here are the blissful downs and dales,
And merrily, merrily carol the gales,
And the spangle dances in bight and bay,
And the rainbow forms and flies on the land
Over the islands free;

And the rainbow lives in the curve of the sand;
Hither, come hither and see;
And the rainbow hangs on the poising wave,
And sweet is the color of cove and cave,
And sweet shall your welcome be.
O, hither, come hither, and be our lords,
For merry brides are we.
We will kiss sweet kisses, and speak sweet words;
O, listen, listen, your eyes shall glisten
With pleasure and love and jubilee.
O, listen, listen, your eyes shall glisten
When the sharp clear twang of the golden chords
Runs up the ridged sea.
Who can light on as happy a shore
All the world o'er, all the world o'er?
Whither away? listen and stay; mariner, mariner, fly no more.

THE
FAERY CHASM

WILLIAM WORDSWORTH

૭૨૦

No fiction was it of the antique age:
A sky-blue stone, within this sunless cleft,
Is of the very footmarks unbereft
Which tiny Elves impressed; — on that smooth stage

Dancing with all their brilliant equipage
In secret revels — haply after theft
Of some sweet Babe — Flower stolen, and coarse Weed left
For the distracted Mother to assuage

Her grief with, as she might! — But, where, oh! where
Is traceable a vestige of the notes
That ruled those dances wild in character? —
Deep underground? Or in the upper air,
On the shrill wind of midnight? or where floats
O'er twilight fields the autumnal gossamer?

from NYMPHIDIA

MICHAEL DRAYTON

But let us leave Queen Mab a while,
Through many a gate, o'er many a stile,
That now had gotten by this wile,
    Her dear Pigwiggen kissing;
And tell how Oberon doth fare,
Who grew as mad as any hare,
When he had sought each place with care,
    And found his queen was missing.
By grisly Pluto he doth swear,
He rent his clothes, and tore his hair,
And as he runneth here and there,
    An acorn-cup he greeteth;
Which soon he taketh by the stalk,
About his head he lets it walk,
Nor doth he any creature balk,
    But lays on all he meeteth.
The Tuscan poet doth advance
The frantic Paladine of France,
And those more ancient do enhance
    Alcides in his fury,
And others Ajax Telamon:
But to this time there hath been none
So bedlam as our Oberon,
    Of which I dare assure you.
And first encount'ring with a wasp,
He in his arms the fly doth clasp,
As tho' his breath he forth would grasp,
    Him for Pigwiggen taking:
'Where is my wife, thou rogue?" quoth he,
"Pigwiggen, she is come to thee,

* * *

Restore her, or thou di'st by me."
Whereat the poor wasp quaking,
Cries, "Oberon, great Fairy King,
Content thee, I am no such thing;
I am a wasp, behold my sting!"
At which the fairy started;
When soon away the wasp doth go,
Poor wretch was never frighted so,
He thought his wings were much too slow,
O'erjoy'd they so were parted.
He next upon a glow-worm light,
(You must suppose it now was night)
Which, for her hinder part was bright,
He took to be a devil,
And furiously doth her assail
For carrying fire in her tail;
He thrash'd her rough coat with his flail,
The mad king fear'd no evil.
"Oh!" quoth the glow-worm "hold thy hand,
Thou puissant King of Fairy-land,
Thy mighty strokes who may withstand?
Hold, or of life despair I."
Together then herself doth roll,
And tumbling down into a hole,
She seem'd as black as any coal,
Which vext away the fairy.
From thence he ran into a hive,
Amongst the bees he letteth drive,
And down their combs begins to rive,
All likely to have spoiled:
Which with their wax his face besmear'd,
And with their honey daub'd his beard;
It would have made a man afear'd,
To see how he was moiled.
A new adventure him betides:
He met an ant, which he bestrides,

And post thereon away he rides,
Which with his haste doth stumble,
And came full over on her snout,
Her heels so threw the dirt about,
For she by no means could get out,
But over him doth tumble.
And being in this piteous case,
And all beslurried head and face,
On runs he in this wildgoose chase;
As here and there he rambles,
Half-blind, against a mole-hill hit,
And for a mountain taking it,
For all he was out of his wit,
Yet to the top he scrambles.
And being gotten to the top,
Yet there himself he could not stop,
But down on th' other side doth chop,
And to the foot came rumbling:
So that the grubs therein that bred,
Hearing such turmoil overhead,
Thought surely they had all been dead,
So fearful was the jumbling.
And falling down into a lake,
Which him up to the neck doth take,
His fury it doth somewhat slake,
He calleth for a ferry:
Where you may some recovery note,
What was his club he made his boat,
And in his oaken cup doth float,
As safe as in a wherry.
Men talk of the adventures strange
Of Don Quishott, and of their change,
Through which he armed oft did range,
Of Sancha Pancha's travel:
But should a man tell every thing,
Done by this frantic fairy king,
And them in lofty numbers sing, it well his wits might gravel.

FAUN

ROBERT GRAVES

Here down this very way,
Here only yesterday
King Faun went leaping.
He sang, with careless shout
Hurling his name about;
He sang, with oaken stock
His steps from rock to rock
In safety keeping,
"Here Faun is free,
Here Faun is free!"

Today against yon pine,
Forlorn yet still divine,
King Faun leant weeping.
"They drank my holy brook,
My strawberries they took,
My private path they trod."
Loud wept the desolate God,
Scorn on scorn heaping,
"Faun, what is he,
Faun, what is he?"

FAIRY REVELS

ANNE HUNTER

A SONG.

HARK, the raven flaps his wings,
The owlet leaves her oaken bower,
Now we dance in airy ring,
On mossy banks at ev'ning hour:
And lightly beat the dewy ground
With our tiny feet around.

Vapours dark, or sprites impure,
Our fairy revels ne'er invade,
In the hawthorn brake secure
The glow-worm lights us thro' the shade.
We lightly beat the dewy ground
With our tiny feet around.

MOON FAIRIES

MADISON JULIUS CAWEIN

൭൨

The moon, a circle of gold,
O'er the crowded housetops rolled,
And peeped in an attic, where,
'Mid sordid things and bare,
A sick child lay and gazed
At a road to the far-away,
A road he followed, mazed,
That grew from a moonbeam-ray,
A road of light that led
From the foot of his garret-bed
Out of that room of hate,
Where Poverty slept by his mate,
Sickness out of the street,
Into a wonderland,
Where a voice called, far and sweet,
"Come, follow our Fairy band!"
A purple shadow, sprinkled
With golden star-dust, twinkled
Suddenly into the room
Out of the winter gloom:
And it wore a face to him
Of a dream he'd dreamed: a form
Of Joy, whose face was dim,
Yet bright with a magic charm.

And the shadow seemed to trail,
Sounds that were green and frail:
Dew-dripples; notes that fell
Like drops in a ferny dell;
A whispered lisp and stir,
Like winds among the leaves,
Blent with a cricket-chirr,
And coo of a dove that grieves.
And the Elfin bore on its back
A little faery pack
Of forest scents: of loam
And mossy sounds of foam;
And of its contents breathed
As might a clod of ground
Feeling a bud unsheathed
There in its womb profound.
And the shadow smiled and gazed
At the child; then softly raised
Its arms and seemed to grow
To a tree in the attic low:
And from its glimmering hands
Shook emerald seeds of dreams,
From which grew fairy bands,
Like firefly motes and gleams.
The child had seen them before
In his dreams of Fairy lore:
The Elves, each with a light
To guide his feet a-right,
Out of this world to a world
Where Magic built him towers,
And Fable old, unfurled,
Flags like wonderful flowers.

* * *

And the child, who knew this, smiled,
And rose, a different child:
No more he knew of pain,
Or fear of heart and brain.
At Poverty there that slept
He never even glanced,
But into the moon-road stept,
And out of the garret danced.
Out of the earthly gloom,
Out of the sordid room,
Out, on a moonbeam ray!
Now at last to play
There with comrades found!
Children of the moon,
There on faery ground,
Where none would find him soon!

ROBIN GOODFELLOW

UNKNOWN

By wells and rills, in meadows green,
We nightly dance our heyday guise;
And to our fairy king and queen,
We chant our moonlight minstrelsies.
When larks 'gin sing,
Away we fling;
And babes new born steal as we go;
And elf in bed
We leave in stead,
And wend us laughing, ho, ho, ho!

From hag-bred Merlin's time, have I
Thus nightly revelled to and fro;
And for my pranks men call me by
The name of Robin Good-fellow.
Fiends, ghosts, and sprites,
Who haunt the nights,
The hags and goblins do me know;
And beldames old
My feats have told,
So vale, vale; ho, ho, ho!

THE WEE FOLK

DONALD MACKENZIE

ᗯᕁ

In the knoll that is the greenest,
And the grey cliff side,
And on the lonely ben-top
The wee folk bide;
They'll flit among the heather,
And trip upon the brae —
The wee folk, the green folk, the red folk and grey.
As o'er the moor at midnight
The wee folk pass,
They whisper 'mong the rushes
And o'er the green grass;
All through the marshy places
They glint and pass away —
The light folk, the lone folk, the folk that will not stay.
O many a fairy milkmaid
With the one eye blind,
Is 'mid the lonely mountains
By the red deer hind;
Not one will wait to greet me,
For they have naught to say —
The hill folk, the still folk, the folk that flit away.
When the golden moon is glinting
In the deep, dim wood,
There's a fairy piper playing
To the elfin brood;
They dance and shout and turn about,
And laugh and swing and sway —
The droll folk, the knoll folk, the folk that dance alway.
O we that bless the wee folk

Have naught to fear,
And ne'er an elfin arrow
Will come us near;
For they'll give skill in music,
And every wish obey —
The wise folk, the peace folk, the folk that work and play.
They'll hasten here at harvest,
They will shear and bind;
They'll come with elfin music
On a western wind;
All night they'll sit among the sheaves,
Or herd the kine that stray —
The quick folk, the fine folk, the folk that ask no pay.
Betimes they will be spinning
The while we sleep,
They'll clamber down the chimney,
Or through keyholes creep;
And when they come to borrow meal
We'll ne'er them send away —
The good folk, the honest folk, the folk that work alway.
O never wrong the wee folk —
The red folk and green,
Nor name them on the Fridays,
Or at Hallowe'en;
The helpless and unwary then
And bairns they lure away —
The fierce folk, the angry folk, the folk that steal and slay.

from
THE CULPRIT FAY

JOSEPH RODMAN DRAKE

He put his acorn helmet on;
It was plumed of the silk of the thistle down;
The corslet plate that guarded his breast
Was once the wild bee's golden vest;
His cloak, of a thousand mingled dyes,
Was formed of the wings of butterflies;
His shield was the shell of a lady-bug green,
Studs of gold on a ground of green;
And the quivering lance which he brandished bright,
Was the sting of a wasp he had slain in fight.
Swift he bestrode his fire-fly steed;
He barred his blade of the bent-grass blue;
He drove his spurs of the cockle-seed,
And away like a glance of thought he flew,
To skim the heavens, and follow far
The fiery trail of the rocket-star.

THE BROWNIES' FEAST

PALMER COX

In best of spirits, blithe and free, —
As Brownies always seem to be, —
A jovial band, with hop and leap,
Were passing through a forest deep,
When in an open space they spied
A heavy caldron, large and wide,

Where woodmen, working at their trade,
A rustic boiling-place had made.
"My friends," said one, "a chance like this
No cunning Brownie band should miss,
All unobserved, we may prepare
And boil a pudding nicely there;
Some dying embers smolder still
Which we may soon revive at will;
And by the roots of yonder tree
A brook goes babbling to the sea.
At Parker's mill, some miles below,
They're grinding flour as white as snow
An easy task for us to bear
Enough to serve our need from there:

I noticed, as I passed to-night,
A window with a broken light,
And through the opening we'll pour
Though bolts and bars be on the door."
"And I," another Brownie cried,
"Will find the plums and currants dried;
I'll have some here in half an hour

* * *

To sprinkle thickly through the flour;
So stir yourselves, and bear in mind
That some must spice and sugar find."
"I know," cried one, "where hens have made
Their nest beneath the burdock shade —
I saw them stealing out with care
To lay their eggs in secret there.
The farmer's wife, through sun and rain,
Has sought to find that nest in vain:
They cackle by the wall of stones,
The hollow stump and pile of bones,
And by the ditch that lies below,
Where yellow weeds and nettles grow;
And draw her after everywhere
Until she quits them in despair.
The task be mine to thither lead
A band of comrades now with speed,
To help me bear a tender load
Along the rough and rugged road."
Away, away, on every side,
At once the lively Brownies glide;
Some after plums, more 'round the hill —
The shortest way to reach the mill —
While some on wings and some on legs
Go darting off to find the eggs.

A few remained upon the spot
To build a fire beneath the pot;
Some gathered bark from trunks of trees,
While others, on their hands and knees,
Around the embers puffed and blew
Until the sparks to blazes grew;
And scarcely was the kindling burned
Before the absent ones returned.
All loaded down they came, in groups,
In couples, singly, and in troops.

Upon their shoulders, heads, and backs
They bore along the floury sacks;
With plums and currants others came,
Each bag and basket filled the same;
While those who gave the hens a call
Had taken nest-egg, nest, and all;
And more, a pressing want to meet,
From some one's line had hauled a sheet,
The monstrous pudding to infold
While in the boiling pot it rolled.
The rogues were flour from head to feet
Before the mixture was complete.
Like snow-birds in a drift of snow
They worked and elbowed in the dough,
Till every particle they brought
Was in the mass before them wrought.
And soon the sheet around the pile
Was wrapped in most artistic style.
Then every plan and scheme was tried
To hoist it o'er the caldron's side.
At times, it seemed about to fall,
Yet none forsook their post through fear,
But harder worked with danger near.
They pulled and hauled and orders gave,
And pushed and pried with stick and stave,
Until, in spite of height and heat,
They had performed the trying feat.
To take the pudding from the pot
They might have found as hard and hot.
But water on the fire they threw,
And then to work again they flew.
And soon the steaming treasure sat
Upon a stone both broad and flat,
Which answered for a table grand,
When nothing better was at hand.

* * *

Some think that Brownies never eat,
But live on odors soft and sweet.
That through the verdant woods proceed
Or steal across the dewy mead;
But those who could have gained a sight
Of them, around their pudding white,
Would have perceived that elves of air
Can relish more substantial fare.
They clustered close, and delved and ate
Without a knife, a spoon, or plate;
Some picking out the plums with care,
And leaving all the pastry there.
While some let plums and currants go,
But paid attention to the dough.
The purpose of each Brownie's mind
Was not to leave a crumb behind,
That, when the morning sun should shine
Through leafy tree and clinging vine,
No traces of their sumptuous feast
It might reveal to man or beast;
And well they gauged what all could bear,
When they their pudding did prepare;
For when the rich repast was done,
The rogues could neither fly nor run.
— The miller never missed his flour,
For Brownies wield a mystic power;
Whate'er they take they can restore
In greater plenty than before.

SONGS OF THE PIXIES

SAMUEL TAYLOR COLERIDGE

༺༻

I. Whom the untaught Shepherds call
Pixies in their madrigal,
Fancy's children, here we dwell:
Welcome, Ladies! to our cell.
Here the wren of softest note
Builds its nest and warbles well;
Here the blackbird strains his throat;
Welcome, Ladies! to our cell.

II. When fades the moon to shadowy-pale,
And scuds the cloud before the gale,
Ere the Morn, all gem-bedight,
Hath streak'd the East with rosy light,
We sip the furze-flower's fragrant dews
Clad in robes of rainbow hues:
Or sport amid the shooting gleams
To the tune of distant-tinkling teams,
While lusty Labour scouting sorrow
Bids the Dame a glad good-morrow,
Who jogs the accustomed road along,
And paces cheery to her cheering song.

III. But not our filmy pinion
We scorch amid the blaze of day,
When Noontide's fiery-tressed minion
Flashes the fervid ray.
Aye from the sultry heat
We to the cave retreat
O'ercanopied by huge roots intertwined

* * *

With wildest texture, blackened o'er with age:
Round them their mantle green the ivies bind,
Beneath whose foliage pale
Fanned by the unfrequent gale
We shield us from the Tyrant's mid-day rage.

IV. Thither, while the murmuring throng
Of wild-bees hum their drowsy song,
By Indolence and Fancy brought,
A youthful Bard, 'unknown to Fame',
Wooes the Queen of Solemn Thought,
And heaves the gentle misery of a sigh
Gazing with tearful eye,
As round our sandy grot appear
Many a rudely sculptured name
To pensive Memory dear!
Weaving gay dreams of sunny-tinctured hue
We glance before his view:
O'er his hush'd soul our soothing witcheries shed
And twine the future garland round his head.

V. When Evening's dusky car
Crowned with her dewy star
Steals o'er the fading sky in shadowy flight;
On leaves of aspen trees
We tremble to the breeze
Veiled from the grosser ken of mortal sight.
Or, haply, at the visionary hour,
Along our wildly-bowered sequestered walk,
We listen to the enamoured rustic's talk;
Heave with the heavings of the maiden's breast,
Where young-eyed Loves have hid their turtle nest;
Or guide of soul-subduing power
The glance, that from the half-confessing eye
Darts the fond question or the soft reply.

VI. Or through the mystic ringlets of the vale
We flash our faery feet in gamesome prank;
Or, silent-sandal'd, pay our defter court,
Circling the Spirit of the Western Gale,
Where wearied with his flower-caressing sport,
Supine he slumbers on a violet bank;
Then with quaint music hymn the parting gleam
By lonely Otter's sleep-persuading stream;
Or where his wave with loud unquiet song
Dashed o'er the rocky channel froths along;
Or where, his silver waters smoothed to rest,
The tall tree's shadow sleeps upon his breast.

VII. Hence thou lingerer, Light!
Eve saddens into Night.
Mother of wildly-working dreams! we view
The sombre hours, that round thee stand
With down-cast eyes (a duteous band!)
Their dark robes dripping with the heavy dew.
Sorceress of the ebon throne!
Thy power the Pixies own,
When round thy raven brow
Heaven's lucent roses glow,
And clouds in watery colours drest
Float in light drapery o'er thy sable vest:
What time the pale moon sheds a softer day
Mellowing the woods beneath its pensive beam:
For mid the quivering light 'tis ours to play,
Aye dancing to the cadence of the stream.

VIII. Welcome, Ladies! to the cell
Where the blameless Pixies dwell:
But thou, sweet Nymph! proclaimed our Faery Queen,
With what obeisance meet
Thy presence shall we greet?

***

For lo! attendant on thy steps are seen
Graceful Ease in artless stole,
And white-robed Purity of soul,
With Honour's softer mien;
Mirth of the loosely-flowing hair,
And meek-eyed Pity eloquently fair,
Whose tearful cheeks are lovely to the view,
As snow-drop wet with dew.

IX. Unboastful Maid! though now the Lily pale
Transparent grace thy beauties meek;
Yet ere again along the impurpling vale,
The purpling vale and elfin-haunted grove,
Young Zephyr his fresh flowers profusely throws,
We'll tinge with livelier hues thy cheek;
And, haply, from the nectar-breathing Rose
Extract a Blush for Love!

NÄCKEN

ERIK JOHAN STAGNELIUS

༄

The evening is festooned with golden clouds
the fairies dance in the meadow
and the leaf-crowned Näcken
plays his fiddle in the silvery brook.

Little boy in the brush on the bank
resting in the violet vapor
hears the noise from the chilly water
calls out in the still night.

"Poor old fellow, why do you play?
will it take the pain away?
you bring the woods and the fields to life
but you'll never be a child of God.

Paradise's moonlit nights
eden's flower-crowned plains
angels of the light on high —
never to be beheld by your eye."

Tears stream down the old man's face
down he dives into the rapids
the fiddle silences.
And the Näcken will never
play again in the silvery brook.

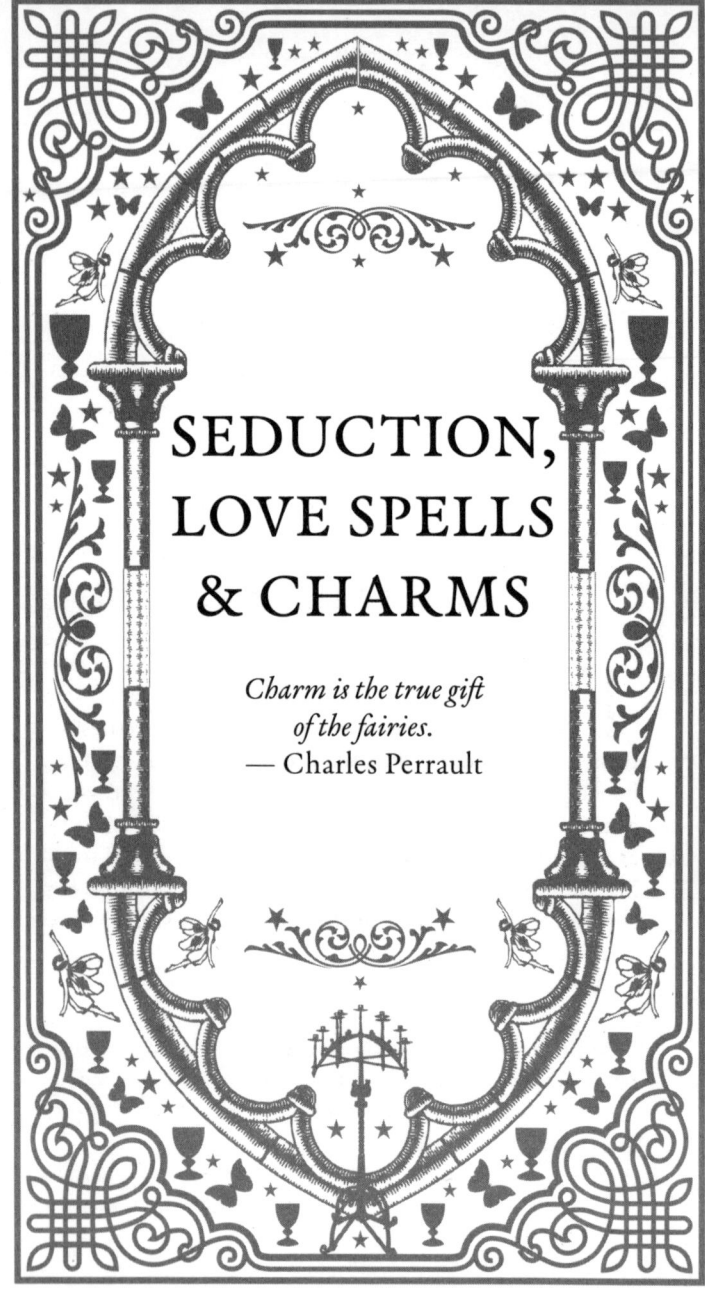

SEDUCTION, LOVE SPELLS & CHARMS

Charm is the true gift of the fairies.
— Charles Perrault

THE ROSE-ELF

HANS CHRISTIAN ANDERSEN

There grew a rose-tree in the middle of a garden; it was quite full of roses; and in one of these, the prettiest of them all, dwelt an elf. He was so very, very small, that no human eye could see him; behind every leaf in the rose he had a sleeping-room; he was as well-formed and as pretty as any child could be, and had wings, which reached from his shoulders down to his feet. O, how fragrant were his chambers, and how bright and beautiful the walls were! They were, indeed, the pale pink, delicate rose leaves.

All day long he enjoyed himself in the warm sunshine, flew from flower to flower, danced upon the wings of the fluttering butterfly, or counted how many paces it was from one footpath to another, upon one single lime leaf. What he considered as footpaths, were what we call veins in the leaf; yes, it was an immense way for him! Before he had finished, the sun had set; thus, he had begun too late.

It became very cold; the dew fell, and the wind blew; the best thing he could do was to get home as fast as he could. He made as much haste as was possible, but all the roses had closed — he could not get in; there was not one single rose open; the poor little elf was quite terrified, he had never been out in the night before; he always had slept in the snug little rose leaf. Now, he certainly would get his death of cold!

At the other end of the garden he knew that there was an arbor, all covered with beautiful honeysuckle. The flowers looked like exquisitely painted horns; he determined to creep down into one of these, and sleep there till morning.

He flew thither. Listen! There are two people within the bower; the one, a handsome young man, and the other, the loveliest young lady that ever was seen; they sat side by side, and wished that they never might be parted, through all eternity. They loved each other very dearly, more dearly than the best child can love either its father or mother.

They kissed each other; and the young lady wept, and gave him a rose; but before she gave it to him she pressed it to her lips, and that with such a deep tenderness, that the rose opened, and the little elf flew into it, and nestled down into its fragrant chamber. As he lay there, he could very plainly hear that they said, — Farewell! farewell! to each other; and then he felt that the rose had its place on the young man's breast. Oh! how his heart beat! — the little elf could not go to sleep because the young man's heart beat so much.

The rose lay there; the young man took it forth whilst he went through a dark wood, and kissed it with such vehemence that the little elf was almost crushed to death; he could feel, through the leaves, how warm were the young man's lips, and the rose gave forth its odor, as if to the noon-day's sun.

Then came another man through the wood; he was dark and wrathful, and was the handsome young lady's cruel brother. He drew forth from its sheath a long and sharp dagger, and whilst the young man kissed the rose, the wicked man stabbed him to death, and then buried him in the bloody earth, under a lime tree.

"Now he is gone and forgotten!" thought the wicked man; "he will never come back again. He is gone a long journey over mountains and seas; it would be an easy thing for him to lose his life, — and he has done so! He will never come back again, and I fancy my sister will never ask after him."

He covered the troubled earth, in which he had laid the dead body, with withered leaves, and then set off home again, through the dark night; but he went not alone, as he fancied; the little elf went with him; it sat in a withered, curled-up lime leaf, which had fallen upon the hair of the cruel man as he dug the grave. He had now put his hat on, and, within, it was very dark; and the little elf trembled with horror and anger over the wicked deed.

In the early hour of morning he came home; he took off his hat, and went into his sister's chamber; there lay the beautiful, blooming maiden, and dreamed about the handsome young man. She loved him very dearly, and thought that now he went over mountains and through woods. The cruel brother bent over her; what were his thoughts we know not, but they must have been evil. The withered lime leaf fell from his hair down upon the bed cover, but he did not notice it; and so he went out, that he, too, might sleep a little in the morning hour.

But the elf crept out of the withered leaf, crept to the ear of the sleeping maiden, and told her, as if in a dream, of the fearful murder; described to her the very place where he had been stabbed, and where his body lay; it told about the blossoming lime tree close beside, and said, — "And that thou mayest not fancy that this is a dream which I tell thee, thou wilt find a withered lime leaf upon thy bed!"

And she found it when she woke.

Oh! what salt tears she wept, and she did not dare to tell her sorrow to any one. The window stood open all day, and the little elf could easily go out into the garden, to the roses and all the other flowers; but for all that, he resolved not to leave the sorrowful maiden.

In the window there stood a monthly rose, and he placed himself in one of its flowers, and there could be near the poor young lady who was so unhappy. Her brother came often into her room, but she could not say one word about the great sorrow of her heart.

As soon as it was night she stole out of the house, went to the wood, and to the very place where the lime tree stood; tore away the dead leaves from the sod, dug down, and found him who was dead! Oh! how she wept and prayed our Lord, that she, too, might soon die!

Gladly would she have taken the body home with her, — but that she could not; so she cut away a beautiful lock of his hair, and laid it near her heart!

Not a word she said; and when she had laid earth and leaves again upon the dead body, she went home; and took with her a little jasmine tree, which grew, full of blossoms, in the wood where he had met with his death.

As soon as she returned to her chamber, she took a very pretty flower-pot, and, filling it with mould, laid in it the beautiful curling hair, and planted in it the jasmine tree.

"Farewell, farewell!" whispered the little elf; he could no longer bear to see her grief, so he flew out into the garden, to his rose; but its leaves had fallen; nothing remained of it but the four green calix leaves.

"Ah! how soon it is over with all that is good and beautiful!" sighed he. At last he found a rose, — which became his house; he crept among its fragrant leaves, and dwelt there.

Every morning he flew to the poor young lady's window, and there she always stood by the flower-pot, and wept. Her salt tears fell upon the jasmine twigs, and every day, as she grew paler and paler, they became more fresh and green; one cluster of flower-buds grew after another; and then the small white buds opened into flowers, and she kissed them. Her cruel brother scolded her, and asked her whether she had lost her senses. He could not imagine why she always wept over that flower-pot, but he did not know what secret lay within its dark mould. But she knew it; she bowed her head over the jasmine bloom, and sank exhausted on her couch. The little rose-elf found her thus, and, stealing to her ear he whispered to her about the evening in the honeysuckle arbor, about the rose's fragrance, and the love which he, the little elf, had for her. She dreamed so sweetly, and while she dreamed, the beautiful angel of death conveyed her spirit away from this world, and she was in heaven with him who was so dear to her.

The jasmine buds opened their large white flowers; their fragrance was wondrously sweet.

When the cruel brother saw the beautiful blossoming tree, he took it, as an heir-loom of his sister, and set it in his sleeping-room, just beside his bed, for it was pleasant to look at, and the fragrance was so rich and uncommon. The little rose-elf went with it, and flew from blossom to blossom. In every blossom there dwelt a little spirit, and to it he told about the murdered young man, whose beautiful curling locks lay under their roots; told about the cruel brother, and the heart-broken sister.

"We know all about it," said the little spirit of each flower; "we know it! we know it! we know it!" and with that they nodded very knowingly.

The rose-elf could not understand them, nor why they seemed so merry, so he flew out to the bees which collected honey, and told them all the story. The bees told it to their queen, who gave orders that, the next morning, they should all go and stab the murderer to death with their sharp little daggers; for that seemed the right thing to the queen-bee.

But that very night, which was the first night after the sister's death, as the brother slept in his bed, beside the fragrant jasmine tree, every little flower opened itself, and all invisibly came forth the spirits of the flower, each with a poisoned arrow; first of all they seated themselves by his ear, and sent such awful dreams to his brain as made him, for the first time, tremble at the deed he had done. They then shot at him with their invisible poisoned arrows.

"Now we have avenged the dead!" said they, and flew back to the white cups of the jasmine-flowers.

As soon as it was morning, the window of the chamber was opened, and in came the rose-elf, with the queen of the bees and all her swarm.

But he was already dead; there stood the people round about his bed, and they said — "That the strong-scented jasmine had been the death of him!"

Then did the rose-elf understand the revenge which the flowers had taken, and he told it to the queen-bee, and she came buzzing, with all her swarm, around the jasmine-pot.

The bees were not to be driven away; so one of the servants took up the pot to carry it out, and one of the bees stung him, and he let the pot fall, and it was broken in two.

Then they all saw the beautiful hair of the murdered young man; and so they knew that he who lay in the bed was the murderer.

The queen-bee went out humming into the sunshine, and she sung about how the flowers had avenged the young man's death; and that behind every little flower-leaf is an eye which can see every wicked deed.

Old and young, think on this! and so, Fare ye well.

THE SONG OF WANDERING AENGUS

W B YEATS

୬୧

I went out to the hazel wood,
Because a fire was in my head,
And cut and peeled a hazel wand,
And hooked a berry to a thread;
And when white moths were on the wing,
And moth-like stars were flickering out,
I dropped the berry in a stream
And caught a little silver trout.
When I had laid it on the floor
I went to blow the fire aflame,
But something rustled on the floor,
And some one called me by my name:
It had become a glimmering girl
With apple blossom in her hair
Who called me by my name and ran
And faded through the brightening air.
Though I am old with wandering
Through hollow lands and hilly lands.
I will find out where she has gone,
And kiss her lips and take her hands;
And walk among long dappled grass,
And pluck till time and times are done
The silver apples of the moon,
The golden apples of the sun.

LA BELLE DAME SANS MERCI

JOHN KEATS

O what can ail thee, knight-at-arms,
　　Alone and palely loitering?
The sedge has withered from the lake,
　　And no birds sing.
O what can ail thee, knight-at-arms,
　　So haggard and so woe-begone?
The squirrel's granary is full,
　　And the harvest's done.
I see a lily on thy brow,
　　With anguish moist and fever-dew,
And on thy cheeks a fading rose
　　Fast withereth too.
I met a lady in the meads,
　　Full beautiful — a faery's child,
Her hair was long, her foot was light,
　　And her eyes were wild.
I made a garland for her head,
　　And bracelets too, and fragrant zone;
She looked at me as she did love,
　　And made sweet moan
I set her on my pacing steed,
　　And nothing else saw all day long,
For sidelong would she bend, and sing
　　A faery's song.
She found me roots of relish sweet,
　　And honey wild, and manna-dew,
And sure in language strange she said —
　　'I love thee true'.

She took me to her Elfin grot,
And there she wept and sighed full sore,
And there I shut her wild wild eyes
With kisses four.
And there she lullèd me asleep,
And there I dreamed — Ah! woe betide! —
The latest dream I ever dreamt
On the cold hill side.
I saw pale kings and princes too,
Pale warriors, death-pale were they all;
They cried — 'La Belle Dame sans Merci
Thee hath in thrall!'
I saw their starved lips in the gloom,
With horrid warning gapèd wide,
And I awoke and found me here,
On the cold hill's side.
And this is why I sojourn here,
Alone and palely loitering,
Though the sedge is withered from the lake,
And no birds sing.

THRICE TOSS THESE OAKEN ASHES

THOMAS CAMPION

Thrice toss these oaken ashes in the air,
Thrice sit thou mute in this enchanted chair;
Then thrice three times tie up this true love's knot,
And murmur soft 'She will, or she will not.'

Go burn these poisonous weeds in yon blue fire,
These screech-owl's feathers and this prickling briar,
This cypress gathered at a dead man's grave,
That all thy fears and cares an end may have.

Then come, you fairies! dance with me a round;
Melt her hard heart with your melodious sound.
In vain are all the charms I can devise;
She hath an art to break them with her eyes.

from
TRISTRAM AND ISEULT

MATTHEW ARNOLD

What tale did Iseult to the children say,
Under the hollies, that bright winter's day?
She told them of the fairy-haunted land
Away the other side of Brittany,
Beyond the heaths, edged by the lonely sea;
Of the deep forest-glades of Broce-liande,
Through whose green boughs the golden sunshine creeps,
Where Merlin by the enchanted thorn-tree sleeps.
For here he came with the fay Vivian,
One April, when the warm days first began.
He was on foot, and that false fay, his friend,
On her white palfrey; here he met his end,
In these lone sylvan glades, that April-day.
This tale of Merlin and the lovely fay
Was the one Iseult chose, and she brought clear
Before the children's fancy him and her.

Blowing between the stems, the forest-air
Had loosen'd the brown locks of Vivian's hair,
Which play'd on her flush'd cheek, and her blue eyes
Sparkled with mocking glee and exercise.
Her palfrey's flanks were mired and bathed in sweat,
For they had travell'd far and not stopp'd yet.
A brier in that tangled wilderness
Had scored her white right hand, which she allows
To rest ungloved on her green riding-dress;
The other warded off the drooping boughs.
But still she chatted on, with her blue eyes

* * *

Fix'd full on Merlin's face, her stately prize.
Her 'haviour had the morning's fresh clear grace,
The spirit of the woods was in her face.
She look'd so witching fair, that learned wight
Forgot his craft, and his best wits took flight;
And he grew fond, and eager to obey
His mistress, use her empire as she may.

[…]

Merlin and Vivian stopp'd on the slope's brow,
To gaze on the light sea of leaf and bough
Which glistering plays all round them, lone and mild,
As if to itself the quiet forest smiled.
Upon the brow-top grew a thorn, and here
The grass was dry and moss'd, and you saw clear
Across the hollow; white anemonies
Starr'd the cool turf, and clumps of primroses
Ran out from the dark underwood behind.
No fairer resting-place a man could find.
"Here let us halt," said Merlin then; and she
Nodded, and tied her palfrey to a tree.

They sate them down together, and a sleep
Fell upon Merlin, more like death, so deep.
Her finger on her lips, then Vivian rose,
And from her brown-lock'd head the wimple throws,
And takes it in her hand, and waves it over
The blossom'd thorn-tree and her sleeping lover.
Nine times she waved the fluttering wimple round,
And made a little plot of magic ground.
And in that daisied circle, as men say,
Is Merlin prisoner till the judgment-day;
But she herself whither she will can rove —
For she was passing weary of his love.

THE FAIRY WELL OF LAGNANAY

SAMUEL FERGUSON.

Mournfully, sing mournfully —
"O listen, Ellen, sister dear:
Is there no help at all for me,
But only ceaseless sigh and tear?
Why did not he who left me here,
With stolen hope steal memory?
O listen, Ellen, sister dear,
(Mournfully, sing mournfully) —
I'll go away to Sleamish hill,
I'll pluck the fairy hawthorn-tree,
And let the spirits work their will;
I care not if for good or ill,
So they but lay the memory
Which all my heart is haunting still!
(Mournfully, sing mournfully) —
The Fairies are a silent race,
And pale as lily flowers to see;
I care not for a blanched face,
For wandering in a dreaming place,
So I but banish memory: —
I wish I were with Anna Grace!"
Mournfully, sing mournfully!

Hearken to my tale of woe —
'Twas thus to weeping Ellen Con,
Her sister said in accents low,
Her only sister, Una bawn:
'Twas in their bed before the dawn,

* * *

And Ellen answered sad and slow, —
"Oh Una, Una, be not drawn
(Hearken to my tale of woe) —
To this unholy grief I pray,
Which makes me sick at heart to know,
And I will help you if I may:
— The Fairy Well of Lagnanay —
Lie nearer me, I tremble so, —
Una, I've heard wise women say
(Hearken to my tale of woe) —
That if before the dews arise,
True maiden in its icy flow
With pure hand bathe her bosom thrice,
Three lady-brackens pluck likewise,
And three times round the fountain go,
She straight forgets her tears and sighs."
Hearken to my tale of woe!

All, alas! and well-away!
"Oh, sister Ellen, sister sweet,
Come with me to the hill I pray,
And I will prove that blessed freet!"
They rose with soft and silent feet,
They left their mother where she lay,
Their mother and her care discreet,
(All, alas! and well-away!)
And soon they reached the Fairy Well,
The mountain's eye, clear, cold, and grey,
Wide open in the dreary fell:
How long they stood 'twere vain to tell,
At last upon the point of day,
Bawn Una bares her bosom's swell,
(All, alas! and well-away!)
Thrice o'er her shrinking breasts she laves

The gliding glance that will not stay
Of subtly-streaming fairy waves: —
And now the charm three brackens craves,
She plucks them in their fring'd array: —
Now round the well her fate she braves,
All, alas! and well-away!

Save us all from Fairy thrall!
Ellen sees her face the rim
Twice and thrice, and that is all —
Fount and hill and maiden swim
All together melting dim!
"Una! Una!" thou may'st call,
Sister sad! but lith or limb
(Save us all from Fairy thrall!)
Never again of Una bawn,
Where now she walks in dreamy hall,
Shall eye of mortal look upon!
Oh! can it be the guard was gone,
The better guard than shield or wall?
Who knows on earth save Jurlagh Daune?
(Save us all from Fairy thrall!)
Behold the banks are green and bare,
No pit is here wherein to fall:
Aye — at the fount you well may stare,
But nought save pebbles smooth is there,
And small straws twirling one and all.
Hie thee home, and be thy pray'r,
Save us all from Fairy thrall.

THE BALLAD OF THE FAIRY THORN-TREE

DORA SIGERSON SHORTER

"This is an evil night to go, my sister,
To the thorn-tree across the fairy rath,
Will you not wait till Hallow Eve is over?
For many are the dangers in your path!"
"I may not wait till Hallow Eve is over,
I shall be there before the night is fled,
For, brother, I am weary for my lover,
And I must see him once, alive or dead.
"I've prayed to heaven, but it would not listen,
I'll call thrice in the devil's name to-night,
Be it a live man that shall come to hear me,
Or but a corpse, all clad in snowy white."

She had drawn on her silken hose and garter,
Her crimson petticoat was kilted high,
She trod her way amid the bog and brambles,
Until the fairy-tree she stood near-by.
When first she cried the devil's name so loudly
She listened, but she heard no sound at all;
When twice she cried, she thought from out the darkness
She heard the echo of a light footfall.
When last she cried her voice came in a whisper,
She trembled in her loneliness and fright;
Before her stood a shrouded, mighty figure,
In sombre garments blacker than the night.

"And if you be my own true love," she questioned,
    "I fear you! Speak you quickly unto me."
"O, I am not your own true love," it answered,
    "He drifts without a grave upon the sea."
"If he be dead, then gladly will I follow
    Down the black stairs of death into the grave."
"Your lover calls you for a place to rest him
    From the eternal tossing of the wave."
"I'll make my love a bed both wide and hollow,
    A grave wherein we both may ever sleep."
"What give you for his body fair and slender,
    To draw it from the dangers of the deep?"
"I'll give you both my silver comb and earrings,
    I'll give you all my little treasure store."
"I will but take what living thing comes forward,
    The first to meet you, passing to your door."
"O may my little dog be first to meet me,
    So loose my lover from your dreaded hold."
"What will you give me for the heart that loved you,
    The heart that I hold chained and frozen cold?"
"My own betrothed ring I give you gladly,
    My ring of pearls — and every one a tear!"
"I will but have what other living creature
    That second in your pathway shall appear."
"To buy this heart, to warm my love to living,
    I pray my pony meet me on return."
"And now, for his young soul what will you give me,
    His soul that night and day doth fret and burn?"
"You will not have my silver comb and earrings,
    You will not have my ring of precious stone;
O, nothing have I left to promise to you,
    But give my soul to buy him back his own."

from BALLAD OF TAM LIN

ROBERT BURNS

'If my love were an earthly knight,
   As he's an elfin grey,
I wad na gie my ain true-love
   For nae lord that ye hae.

'The steed that my true-love rides on
   Is lighter than the wind;
Wi siller he is shod before,
   Wi burning gowd behind.'

Janet has kilted her green kirtle
   A little aboon her knee,
And she has snooded her yellow hair
   A little aboon her bree,
And she's awa to Carterhaugh,
   As fast as she can hie.

When she cam to Carterhaugh,
   Tam Lin was at the well,
And there she fand his steed standing,
   But away was himsel.

She had na pu'd a double rose,
   A rose but only twa,
Till up then started young Tam Lin,
   Says Lady, thou pu's nae mae.

Why pu's thou the rose, Janet,
   Amang the groves sae green,
And a' to kill the bonie babe
   That we gat us between?

'O tell me, tell me, Tam Lin,' she says,
    'For's sake that died on tree,
  If eer ye was in holy chapel,
    Or christendom did see?'

'Roxbrugh he was my grandfather,
    Took me with him to bide,
  And ance it fell upon a day
    That wae did me betide.

'And ance it fell upon a day,
    A cauld day and a snell,
When we were frae the hunting come,
    That frae my horse I fell;
The Queen o Fairies she caught me,
    In yon green hill to dwell.
'And pleasant is the fairy land,
    But, an eerie tale to tell,
Ay at the end of seven years
    We pay a tiend to hell;
I am sae fair and fu o flesh,
    I'm feard it be myself.

'But the night is Halloween, lady,
    The morn is Hallowday;
Then win me, win me, an ye will,
    For weel I wat ye may.

'Just at the mirk and midnight hour
    The fairy folk will ride,
And they that wad their true-love win,
    At Miles Cross they maun bide.'

MY FAIRY LOVER

DONALD A. MACKENZIE

My fairy lover, my fairy lover,
My fair, my rare one, come back to me —
All night I'm sighing, for thee I'm crying,
I would be dying, my love, for thee.

Thine eyes were glowing like blue-bells blowing,
With dew-drops twinkling their silvery fires;
Thine heart was panting with love enchanting,
For mine was granting its fond desires.

My fairy lover, my fairy lover,
My fair, my rare one, come back to me —
All night I'm sighing, for thee I'm crying,
I would be dying, my love, for thee.

Thy brow had brightness and lily-whiteness,
Thy cheeks were clear as yon crimson sea;
Like broom-buds gleaming, thy locks were streaming,
As I lay dreaming, my love, of thee.

My fairy lover, my fairy lover,
My fair, my rare one, come back to me —
All night I'm sighing, for thee I'm crying,
I would be dying, my love, for thee.

Thy lips that often with love would soften,
They beamed like blooms for the honey-bee;
Thy voice came ringing like some bird singing
When thou wert bringing thy gifts to me.

My fairy lover, my fairy lover,
My fair, my rare one, come back to me —
All night I'm sighing, for thee I'm crying,
I would be dying, my love, for thee.

O thou'rt forgetting the hours we met in
The Vale of Tears at the even-tide,
Or thou'd come near me to love and cheer me,
And whisper clearly, "O be my bride!"

My fairy lover, my fairy lover,
My fair, my rare one, come back to me —
All night I'm sighing, for thee I'm crying,
I would be dying, my love, for thee.

What spell can bind thee? I search to find thee
Around the knoll that thy home would be —
Where thou did'st hover, my fairy lover,
The clods will cover and comfort me.

My fairy lover, my fairy lover,
My fair, my rare one, come back to me —
All night I'm sighing, on thee I'm crying,
I would be dying, my love, for thee.

THE BALLAD OF SIR OLOF IN THE ELVE-DANCE

THOMAS KEIGHTLEY

Sir Olof he rode out at early day,
And so came he unto an Elve-dance gay.
    The dance it goes well,
    So well in the grove.

The Elve-father reached out his white hand free,
"Come, come, Sir Olof, tread the dance with me."
    The dance it goes well,
    So well in the grove.

"O nought I will, and nought I may,
To-morrow will be my wedding-day."
    The dance it goes well,
    So well in the grove.

And the Elve-mother reached out her white hand free,
"Come, come, Sir Olof, tread the dance with me."
    The dance it goes well,
    So well in the grove.

"O nought I will, and nought I may,
To-morrow will be my wedding-day."
    The dance it goes well,
    So well in the grove.

And the Elve-sister reached out her white hand free,
"Come, come, Sir Olof, tread the dance with me."
    The dance it goes well,
    So well in the grove.

"O nought I will, and nought I may,
To-morrow will be my wedding-day."
    The dance it goes well,
    So well in the grove.

And the bride she spake with her bride-maids so,
"What may it mean that the bells thus go?"
    The dance it goes well,
    So well in the grove.

"'Tis the custom of this our isle," they replied;
"Each young swain ringeth home his bride."
    The dance it goes well,
    So well in the grove.

"And the truth from you to conceal I fear,
Sir Olof is dead, and lies on his bier."
    The dance it goes well,
    So well in the grove.

And on the morrow, ere light was the day,
In Sir Olof's house three corpses lay.
    The dance it goes well,
    So well in the grove.

It was Sir Olof, his bonny bride,
And eke his mother, of sorrow she died.
    The dance it goes well,
    So well in the grove.

MISCHIEF & MALEVOLENCE

Do not think the fairies are always little. Everything is capricious about them, even their size. They seem to take what size or shape pleases them.
— W B Yeats

from
THE FAIRY FLEET

GEORGE MACDONALD

The bed was about a couple of yards from the edge of the brook. And as Colin was always first up in the morning, he slept at the front of the bed. So he lay for some time gazing at the faint glimmer of the water in the dull red light from the sod-covered fire, and listening to its sweet music as it hurried through to the night again, till its murmur changed into a lullaby, and sung him fast asleep.

Soon he found that he was coming awake again. He was lying listening to the sound of the busy stream. But it had gathered more sounds since he went to sleep-amongst the rest, one of boards knocking together, and a tiny chattering and sweet laughter, like the tinkling of heather-bells. He opened his eyes. The moon was shining along the brook, lighting the smoky rafters above with its reflection from the water, which had been dammed back at its outlet from the cottage, so that it lay bank-full and level with the floor. But its surface was hardly to be seen, save by an occasional glimmer, for the crowded boats of a fairy fleet which had just arrived. The sailors were as busy as sailors could be, mooring along the banks, or running their boats high and dry on the shore. Some had little sails which glimmered white in the moonshine-half-lowered, or blowing out in the light breeze that crept down the course of the stream. Some were pulling about through the rest, oars flashing, tiny voices calling, tiny feet running, tiny hands hauling at ropes that ran through blocks of shining ivory. On the shore stood groups of fairy ladies in all colours of the rainbow, green predominating, waited upon by gentlemen all in green, but with red and yellow feathers in their caps. The queen had landed on the side next to Colin, and in a few minutes more twenty dances were going at once along the shores of the fairy river. And there lay great Colin's face, just above the bed-clothes, glowering at them like an ogre.

At last, after a few dances, he heard a clear sweet, ringing voice say,

"I've had enough of this. I'm tired of doing like the big people. Let's have a game of Hey Cockolorum Jig!"

That instant every group sprang asunder, and every fairy began a frolic on his own account. They scattered all over the cottage, and Colin lost sight of most of them.

While he lay watching the antics of two of those near him, who behaved more like clowns at a fair than the gentlemen they had been a little while before, he heard a voice close to his ear; but though he looked everywhere about his pillow, he could see nothing. The voice stopped the moment he began to look, but began again as soon as he gave it up.

"You can't see me. I'm talking to you through a hole in the head of your bed.

"Don't look," said the voice. "If the queen sees me I shall be pinched. Oh, please don't."

The voice sounded as if its owner would cry presently. So Colin took good care not to look. It went on:

"Please, I am a little girl, not a fairy. The queen stole me the minute I was born, seven years ago, and I can't get away. I don't like the fairies. They are so silly. And they never grow any wiser. I grow wiser every year. I want to get back to my own people. They won't let me. They make me play at being somebody else all night long, and sleep all day. That's what they do themselves. And I should so like to be myself. The queen says that's not the way to be happy at all; but I do want very much to be a little girl. Do take me."

"How am I to get you?" asked Colin in a whisper, which sounded, after the sweet voice of the changeling, like the wind in a field of dry beans.

"The queen is so pleased with you that she is sure to offer you something. Choose me. Here she comes."

Immediately he heard another voice, shriller and stronger, in front of him; and, looking about, saw standing on the edge of the bed a lovely little creature, with a crown glittering with jewels, and a rush for a sceptre in her hand, the blossom of which shone like a bunch of garnets.

"You great staring creature!" she said. "Your eyes are much too big to see with. What clumsy hobgoblins you thick folk are!"

So saying, she laid her wand across Colin's eyes.

"Now, then, stupid!" she said and that instant Colin saw the room like a huge barn, full of creatures about two feet high. The beams overhead were crowded with fairies, playing all imaginable tricks, scrambling everywhere, knocking each other over, throwing dust and soot in each other's faces, grinning from behind corners, dropping on each other's necks, and tripping up each other's heels. Two had got hold of an empty egg-shell, and coming behind one sitting on the edge of the table, and laughing at some one on the floor, tumbled it right over him, so that he was lost in the cavernous hollow. But the lady-fairies mingled in none of these rough pranks. Their tricks were always graceful, and they had more to say than to do.

But the moment the queen had laid her wand across his eyes, she went on:

"Know, son of a human mortal, that thou hast pleased a queen of the fairies. Lady as I am over the elements I cannot have everything I desire. One thing thou hast given me. Years have I longed for a path down this rivulet to the ocean below. Your horrid farm-yard, ever since your great-grandfather built this cottage, was the one obstacle. For we fairies hate dirt, not only in houses, but in fields and woods as well, and above all in running streams. But I can't talk like this any longer. I tell you what, you are a dear good boy, and you shall have what you please. Ask me for anything you like."

"May it please your majesty," said Colin, very deliberately, "I want a little girl that you carried away some seven years ago the moment she was born. May it please your majesty, I want her."

"It does not please my majesty," cried the queen, whose face had been growing very black. "Ask for something else "

"Then, whether it pleases your majesty or not," said Colin, bravely, "I hold your majesty to your word. I want that little girl, and that little girl I will have and nothing else."

"You dare to talk so to me, you thick!"

"Yes, your majesty."

"Then you sha'n't have her."

"Then I'll turn the brook right through the dunghill," said Colin. "Do you think I'll let you come into my cottage to play at high jinks when you please, if you behave to me like this?"

And Colin sat up in bed, and looked the queen in the face. And as he did so he caught sight of the loveliest little creature peeping round the corner at the foot of the bed. And he knew she was the little girl because she was quiet, and looked frightened, and was sucking her thumb.

Then the queen, seeing with whom she had to deal, and knowing that queens in Fairyland are bound by their word, began to try another plan with him. She put on her sweetest manner and looks; and as she did so, the little face at the foot of the bed grew more troubled, and the little head shook itself, and the little thumb dropped out of the little mouth.

"Dear Colin," said the queen, "you shall have the girl. But you must do something for me first."

The little girl shook her head as fast as ever she could, but Colin was taken up with the queen.

"To be sure I will. What is it?" he said.

And so he was bound by a new bargain, and was in the queen's power.

"You must fetch me a bottle of Carasoyn," said she.

"What is that?" asked Colin.

"A kind of wine that makes people happy."

"Why, are you not happy already?"

"No, Colin," answered the queen, with a sigh.

"You have everything you want."

"Except the Carasoyn," returned the queen.

"You do whatever you like, and go wherever you please."

"That's just it. I want something that I neither like nor please-that I don't know anything about. I want a bottle of Carasoyn."

And here she cried like a spoilt child, not like a sorrowful woman.

"But how am I to get it?"

"I don't know. You must find out."

"Oh! that's not fair," cried Colin.

But the queen burst into a fit of laughter that sounded like the bells of a hundred frolicking sheep, and bounding away to the side of the river, jumped on board of her boat. And like a swarm of bees gathered the courtiers and sailors; two creeping out of the bellows, one at the nozzle and the other at the valve; three out of the basket-hilt of the broadsword on the wall; six all white out of the meal-tub; and so from all parts of the cottage to the river-side. And amongst them Colin spied the little girl creeping on board the queen's boat, with her pinafore to her eyes; and the queen was shaking her fist at her. In five minutes more they had all scrambled into the boats, and the whole fleet was in motion down the stream. In another moment the cottage was empty, and everything had returned to its usual size.

"They'll be all dashed to pieces on the rocks," cried Colin, jumping up, and running into the garden. When he reached the fall, there was nothing to be seen but the swift plunge and rush of the broken water in the moonlight. He thought he heard cries and shouts coming up from below, and fancied he could distinguish the sobs of the little maiden whom he had so foolishly lost. But the sounds might be only those of the water, for to the different voices of a running stream there is no end. He followed its course all the way to its old channel, but saw nothing to indicate any disaster. Then he crept beck to his bed, where he lay thinking what a fool he had been, till he cried himself to sleep over the little girl who would never grow into a woman.

THE CHANGELING

CHARLOTTE MEW

Toll no bell for me, dear Father, dear Mother,
　　Waste no sighs;
There are my sisters, there is my little brother
　　Who plays in the place called Paradise,
　　Your children all, your children for ever;
　　　　But I, so wild,
Your disgrace, with the queer brown face, was never,
　　Never, I know, but half your child!
In the garden at play, all day, last summer,
　　Far and away I heard
The sweet "tweet-tweet" of a strange new-comer,
　　The dearest, clearest call of a bird.
It lived down there in the deep green hollow,
　　My own old home, and the fairies say
The word of a bird is a thing to follow,
　　So I was away a night and a day.
One evening, too, by the nursery fire,
　　We snuggled close and sat round so still,
When suddenly as the wind blew higher,
　　Something scratched on the window-sill.
A pinched brown face peered in — I shivered;
　　No one listened or seemed to see;
The arms of it waved and the wings of it quivered,
　　Whoo — I knew it had come for me;
　　Some are as bad as bad can be!
All night long they danced in the rain,
Round and round in a dripping chain,
Threw their caps at the window-pane,
Tried to make me scream and shout

* * *

And fling the bedclothes all about:
I meant to stay in bed that night,
And if only you had left a light
They would never have got me out.
Sometimes I wouldn't speak, you see,
Or answer when you spoke to me,
Because in the long, still dusks of Spring
You can hear the whole world whispering;
The shy green grasses making love,
The feathers grow on the dear, grey dove,
The tiny heart of the redstart beat,
The patter of the squirrel's feet,
The pebbles pushing in the silver streams,
The rushes talking in their dreams,
The swish-swish of the bat's black wings,
The wild-wood bluebell's sweet ting-tings,
Humming and hammering at your ear,
Everything there is to hear
In the heart of hidden things,
But not in the midst of the nursery riot,
That's why I wanted to be quiet
Couldn't do my sums, or sing,
Or settle down to anything.
And when, for that, I was sent upstairs
I did kneel down to say my prayers;
But the King who sits on your high church steeple
Has nothing to do with us fairy people!
'Times I pleased you, dear Father, dear Mother,
Learned all my lessons and liked to play,
And dearly I loved the little pale brother
Whom some other bird must have called away.
Why did They bring me here to make me
Not quite bad and not quite good,
Why, unless They're wicked, do They want, in spite, to take me
Back to their wet, wild wood?

Now, every night I shall see the windows shining, The gold
    lamp's glow, and the fire's red gleam,
While the best of us are twining twigs and the rest of
    us are whining
        In the hollow by the stream.
    Black and chill are Their nights on the wold;
    And They live so long and They feel no pain:
        I shall grow up, but never grow old,
        I shall always, always be very cold,

I SHALL NEVER COME BACK AGAIN!

THE ERL-KING

JOHANN WOLFGANG VON GOETHE

Who rides there so late through the night dark and drear?
The father it is, with his infant so dear;
He holdeth the boy tightly clasp'd in his arm,
He holdeth him safely, he keepeth him warm.

"My son, wherefore seek'st thou thy face thus to hide?"
Look, father, the Erl-King is close by our side!
Dost see not the Erl-King, with crown and with train?"
"My son, 'tis the mist rising over the plain."

"Oh, come, thou dear infant! oh come thou with me!
Full many a game I will play there with thee;
On my strand, lovely flowers their blossoms unfold,
My mother shall grace thee with garments of gold."

"My father, my father, and dost thou not hear
The words that the Erl-King now breathes in mine ear?"
"Be calm, dearest child, 'tis thy fancy deceives;
'Tis the sad wind that sighs through the withering leaves."

"Wilt go, then, dear infant, wilt go with me there?
My daughters shall tend thee with sisterly care
My daughters by night their glad festival keep,

They'll dance thee, and rock thee, and sing thee to sleep."
"My father, my father, and dost thou not see,
How the Erl-King his daughters has brought here for me?"
"My darling, my darling, I see it aright,
'Tis the aged grey willows deceiving thy sight."

"I love thee, I'm charm'd by thy beauty, dear boy!
And if thou'rt unwilling, then force I'll employ."
"My father, my father, he seizes me fast,
Full sorely the Erl-King has hurt me at last."

The father now gallops, with terror half wild,
He grasps in his arms the poor shuddering child;
He reaches his courtyard with toil and with dread,
The child in his arms finds he motionless, dead.

FAIRY TALE

JAMES MCINTYRE

ഗര

Where'er you find the Fisher folk
There, under superstitions yoke,
For a strong faith 'mong them prevails.
Of truth of witch and fairy tales.
They think that witch could hurl a shaft
Which would o'erwhelm their fishing craft,
For witches do with Satan truck,
They can give good or bring bad luck;
Fish women do their children teach
To bait the lines down on the beach ;
Themselves do wade in sea for net
So husband's feet will not get wet,
For the women are barefooted,
And the men are heavy booted.

In Fisher, Town of Cromarty,
There once did meet a noisy party,
Confusion worse than Babel's Tower,
It did prevail for a whole hour;
When from sea shore wives did return
Each one did find good cause to mourn,
For each babe was left in cradle,
Had been changed, 'tis no fable ;

They said 'twas fairies did them change,
And left with them but weaklings strange.
Old wife, to end confusion wild,
Said each must bring to her the child ;
Soon mothers they did find their dears,
And did wipe then from eyes all tears,
While few young men across the way
They glorious did enjoy the fray,
For while the mothers were at beach
They changed all babes within their reach.

WHERE THEY COME UNTO THE FAERY'S COURT

JOHN KEATS

When they were come unto the Faery's court
They rang — no one at home — all gone to sport
And dance and kiss and love as faeries do,
For faeries be as humans, lovers true —
Amid the woods they were, so lone and wild,
Where even the robin feels himself exil'd
And where the very brooks as if afraid
Hurry along to some less magic shade.
"No one at home!" the fretful Princess cry'd
"And all for nothing such a dreary ride,
And all for nothing my new diamond cross,
No one to see my Persian feathers toss,
No one to see my Ape, my Dwarf, my Fool,
Or how I pace my Otaheitan mule.
Ape, Dwarf and Fool, why stand you gaping there?
Burst the door open, quick — or I declare
I'll switch you soundly and in pieces tear."
The Dwarf began to tremble and the Ape
Star'd at the Fool, the Fool was all agape;
The Princess grasp'd her switch, but just in time
The Dwarf with piteous face began to rhyme.
"O mighty Princess, did you ne'er hear tell
What your poor servants know but too, too well?
Know you the three great crimes in faery land?
The first, alas! poor Dwarf, I understand —
I made a whipstock of a faery's wand;
The next is snoring in their company;
The next, the last, the direst of the three,

Is making free when they are not at home.
I was a Prince — a baby Prince — my doom
You see, I made a whipstock of a wand;
My top has henceforth slept in faery land.
He was a Prince, the Fool, a grown up prince,
But he has never been a king's son since
He fell a-snoring at a faery ball.
Your poor Ape was a prince, and he, poor thing,
Picklock'd a faery's boudoir — now no king,
But Ape — so pray your highness stay awhile;
'Tis sooth indeed, we know it to our sorrow —
Persist and you may be an Ape tomorrow "
While the Dwarf spake the princess all for spite
Peel'd the brown hazel twig to lilly white,
Clench'd her small teeth, and held her lips apart,
Try'd to look unconcern'd with beating heart.
They saw her highness had made up her mind,
A quavering like three reeds before the wind —
And they had had it, but, O happy chance,
The Ape for very fear began to dance,
And grinn'd as all his ugliness did ache.
She staid her vixen fingers for his sake,
He was so very ugly: then she took
Her pocket mirror and began to look
First at herself and then at him and then
She smil'd at her own beauteous face again.
Yet for all this — for all her pretty face —
She took it in her head to see the place.

* * *

Women gain little from experience
Either in lovers, husbands, or expence.
The more the beauty, the more fortune too:
Beauty before the wide world never knew —
So each Fair reasons — tho' it oft miscarries.
She thought her pretty face would please the faeries.
"My darling Ape, I won't whip you to-day —
Give me the picklock, sirrah, and go play."
They all three wept — but counsel was as vain
As crying c'up, biddy to drops of rain.
Yet lingeringly did the sad Ape forth draw
The picklock from the pocket in his jaw.
The Princess took it and, dismounting straight,
Tripp'd in blue silver'd slippers to the gate
And touch'd the wards; the door full courteously
Opened — she enter'd with her servants three.
Again it clos'd and there was nothing seen
But the Mule grazing on the herbage green.

THE FAIRIES' DANCE

THOMAS RAVENSCROFT

Dare you haunt our hallow'd green?
None but fairies here are seen.
Down and sleep,
Wake and weep,
Pinch him black, and pinch him blue,
That seeks to steal a lover true!
When you come to hear us sing,
Or to tread our fairy ring,
Pinch him black, and pinch him blue!
O thus our nails shall handle you!

THE FAIRIES

WILLIAM ALLINGHAM

Up the airy mountain,
Down the rushy glen,
We daren't go a-hunting
For fear of little men;
Wee folk, good folk,
Trooping all together;
Green jacket, red cap,
And white owl's feather!

Down along the rocky shore
Some make their home,
They live on crispy pancakes
Of yellow tide-foam;
Some in the reeds
Of the black mountain-lake,
With frogs for their watchdogs,
All night awake.

High on the hill-top
The old King sits;
He is now so old and grey
He's nigh lost his wits.
With a bridge of white mist
Columbkill he crosses,
On his stately journeys
From Slieveleague to Rosses;
Or going up with music
On cold starry nights,
To sup with the Queen
Of the gay Northern Lights.

They stole little Bridget
For seven years long;
When she came down again
Her friends were all gone.
They took her lightly back,
Between the night and morrow,
They thought that she was fast asleep,
But she was dead with sorrow.
They have kept her ever since
Deep within the lake,
On a bed of flag-leaves,
Watching till she wake.

By the craggy hillside,
Through the mosses bare,
They have planted thorn trees
For pleasure, here and there.
Is any man so daring
As dig them up in spite,
He shall find their sharpest thorns
In his bed at night.

Up the airy mountain,
Down the rushy glen,
We daren't go a-hunting
For fear of little men;
Wee folk, good folk,
Trooping all together;
Green jacket, red cap,
And white owl's feather!

THE STOLEN CHILD

W B YEATS

൶

Where dips the rocky highland
Of Sleuth Wood in the lake,
There lies a leafy island
Where flapping herons wake
The drowsy water-rats.
There we've hid our fairy vats
Full of berries,
And of reddest stolen cherries.
Come away, O, human child!
To the woods and waters wild,
With a fairy hand in hand,
For the world's more full of weeping than you can understand.
Where the wave of moonlight glosses
The dim grey sands with light,
Far off by furthest Rosses
We foot it all the night,
Weaving olden dances,
Mingling hands, and mingling glances,
Till the moon has taken flight;
To and fro we leap,
And chase the frothy bubbles,
While the world is full of troubles.
And is anxious in its sleep.
Come away! O, human child!
To the woods and waters wild.
With a fairy hand in hand,

For the world's more full of weeping than you can understand.
Where the wandering water gushes.
From the hills above Glen-Car,
In pools among the rushes,
That scarce could bathe a star,
We seek for slumbering trout,
And whispering in their ears;
We give them evil dreams,
Leaning softly out
From ferns that drop their tears
Of dew on the young streams.
Come! O, human child!
To the woods and waters wild,
With a fairy hand in hand,
For the world's more full of weeping than you can understand.
Away with us, he's going,
The solemn-eyed;
He'll hear no more the lowing
Of the calves on the warm hill-side.
Or the kettle on the hob
Sing peace into his breast;
Or see the brown mice bob
Round and round the oatmeal chest.
For he comes, the human child,
To the woods and waters wild,
With a fairy hand in hand,
For the world's more full of weeping than he can understand.

THE FAIRY THORN

SAMUEL FERGUSON

"Get up, our Anna dear, from the weary spinning wheel;
For your father's on the hill, and your mother is asleep:
Come up above the crags, and we'll dance a highland reel
    Around the fairy thorn on the steep."

At Anna Grace's door 'twas thus the maidens cried,
    Three merry maidens fair in kirtles of the green;
And Anna laid the sock and the weary wheel aside,
    The fairest of the four, I ween.

They're glancing through the glimmer of the quiet eve,
    Away in milky wavings of neck and ankle bare;
The heavy-sliding stream in its sleeply song they leave,
    And the crags in the ghostly air:

And linking hand in hand, and singing as they go,
The maids along the hill-side have ta'en their fearless way,
Till they come to where the rowan trees in lovely beauty
    grow
    Beside the Fairy Hawthorn gray.

The hawthorn stands between the ashes tall and slim,
    Like matron with her twin grand-daughters at her knee;
The rowan berries cluster o'er her low head gray and dim
    In ruddy kisses sweet to see.

The merry maidens four have ranged them in a row,
    Between each lovely couple a stately rowan stem,
And away in mazes wavy like skimming birds they go,
    Oh, never caroll'd bird like them!

But solemn is the silence of the silvery haze
That drinks away their voices in echoless repose,
And dreamily the evening has still'd the haunted braes,
And dreamier the gloaming grows.

And sinking one by one, like lark-notes from the sky
When the falcon's shadow saileth across the open shaw,
Are hush'd the maidens' voices, as cowering down they lie
In the flutter of their sudden awe.

For, from the air above and the grassy ground beneath,
And from the mountain-ashes and the old white thorn between,
A power of faint enchantment doth through their beings breathe,
And they sink down together on the green.

They sink together silent, and, stealing side by side,
They fling their lovely arms o'er their drooping necks so fair,
Then vainly strive again their naked arms to hide,
For their shrinking necks again are bare.

Thus clasp'd and prostrate all, with their heads together bow'd,
Soft o'er their bosoms beating — the only human sound —
They hear the silky footsteps of the silent fairy crowd,
Like a river in the air, gliding round.
Nor scream can any raise, nor prayer can any say,
But wild, wild, the terror of the speechless three —

* * *

For they feel fair Anna Grace drawn silently away,
    By whom they dare not look to see.

They feel their tresses twine with her parting locks of gold,
    And the curls elastic falling, as her head withdraws;
They feel her sliding arms from their tranced arms unfold,
    But they dare not look to see the cause:

For heavy on their senses the faint enchantment lies
    Through all that night of anguish and perilous amaze;
And neither fear nor wonder can ope their quivering eyes,
    Or their limbs from the cold ground raise,

Till out of night the earth has roll'd her dewy side,
    With every haunted mountain and streamy vale below;
When, as the mist dissolves in the yellow morning-tide,
    The maidens' trance dissolveth so.

Then fly the ghastly three as swiftly as they may,
    And tell their tale of sorrow to anxious friends in vain:
They pin'd away and died within the year and day,
    And ne'er was Anna Grace seen again.

THE CHANGELING

DONALD MACKENZIE

By night they came and from my bed
They stole my babe, and left behind
A thing I hate, a thing I dread —
A changeling who is old and blind;
He's moaning all the night and day
For those who took my babe away.
My little babe was sweet and fair,
He crooned to sleep upon my breast —
But O the burden I must bear!
This drinks all day and will not rest —
My little babe had hair so light —
And his is growing dark as night.
Yon evil day when I would leave
My little babe the stook behind! —
The fairies coming home at eve
Upon an eddy of the wind,
Would cast their eyes with envy deep
Upon my heart's-love in his sleep.
What holy woman will ye find
To weave a spell and work a charm?
A holy woman, pure and kind,
Who'll keep my little babe from harm —
Who'll make the evil changeling flee,
And bring my sweet one back to me?

THE FAIRY

WILLIAM BLAKE

ಲ╭ಲ

'COME hither, my Sparrows,
My little arrows.
If a tear or a smile
Will a man beguile,
If an amorous delay
Clouds a sunshiny day,
If the step of a foot
Smites the heart to its root,
'Tis the marriage-ring…
Makes each fairy a king.'

So a Fairy sung.
From the leaves I sprung;
He leap'd from the spray
To flee away;
But in my hat caught,
He soon shall be taught.
Let him laugh, let him cry,
He's my Butterfly;
For I've pull'd out the sting
Of the marriage-ring.

TAM O' SHANTER

ROBERT BURNS

When chapman billies leave the street,
And drouthy neebors neebors meet,
As market-days are wearing late,
An' folk begin to tak the gate;
While we sit bousing at the nappy,
An' getting fou and unco happy,
We think na on the lang Scots miles,
The mosses, waters, slaps, and styles,
That lie between us and our hame,
Whare sits our sulky, sullen dame,
Gathering her brows like gathering storm,
Nursing her wrath to keep it warm.
This truth fand honest Tam O'Shanter,
As he frae Ayr ae night did canter
(Auld Ayr, wham ne'er a town surpasses,
For honest men and bonnie lasses).
O Tam! hadst thou been but sae wise
As taen thy ain wife Kate's advice!
She tauld thee weel thou was a skellum,
A blethering, blustering, drunken blellum:
That frae November till October,
Ae market-day thou was na sober,
That ilka melder, wi' the miller
Thou sat as lang as thou had siller;
That every naig was ca'd a shoe on,
The smith and thee gat roaring fou on;
That at the Lord's house, ev'n on Sunday,
Thou drank wi'Kirton Jean till Monday.

* * *

She prophesied that, late or soon,
Thou would be found deep drowned in Doon;
Or catched wi' warlocks in the mirk,
By Alloway's auld haunted kirk.
Ah, gentle dames! it gars me greet
To think how monie counsels sweet,
How monie lengthened sage advices,
The husband frae the wife despises!
But to our tale: Ae market night
Tam had got planted unco right,
Fast by an ingle, bleezing finely,
Wi' reaming swats, that drank divinely;
And at his elbow souter Johnny,
His ancient, trusty, drouthy crony.
Tam lo'ed him like a vera brither;
They had been fou for weeks thegither.
The night drave on wi' sangs and clatter
And aye the ale was growing better;
The landlady and Tam grew gracious,
Wi' favors secret, sweet, and precious;
The souter tauld his queerest stories;
The landlord's laugh was ready chorus;
The storm without might rair and rustle,
Tam did na mind the storm a whistle.
Care, mad to see a man sae happy,
E'en drowned himself amang the nappy;
As bees flee hame wi' lades o' treasure,
The minutes winged their way wi' pleasure;
Kings may be blest, but Tam was glorious,
O'er a' the ills o' life victorious.
But pleasures are like poppies spread;
You seize the flower, its bloom is shed;
Or like the snow-fall in the river,
A moment white, — then melts forever;
Or like the borealis race,
That flit ere you can point their place;

Or like the rainbow's lovely form
Evanishing amid the storm.
Nae man can tether time or tide;
The hour approaches Tam maun ride;
That hour o'night's black arch the keystane,
That dreary hour he mounts his beast in;
And sic a night he takes the road in
As ne'er poor sinner was abroad in.
The wind blew as 't wad blawn its last;
The rattling showers rose on the blast;
The speedy gleams the darkness swallowed;
Loud, deep, and lang the thunder bellowed;
That night a child might understand
The Deil had business on his hand.
Weel mounted on his gray mare, Meg,
(A better never lifted leg,)
Tam skeppit on thro' dub and mire,
Despising wind and rain and fire,
Whyles holding fast his guid blue bonnet,
Whyles crooning o'er some auld Scots sonnet,
Whyles glowering round wi' prudent cares,
Lest bogles catch him unawares;
Kirk-Alloway was drawing nigh,
Whare ghaists and houlets nightly cry.
By this time he was cross the ford,
Whare in the snaw the chapman smoored;
And past the birks and meikle stane,
Whare drunken Charlie brak's neck-bane;
And through the whins, and by the cairn,
Whare hunters fand the murdered bairn;
And near the thorn, aboon the well,
Whare Mungo's mither hanged hersel'.
Before him Doon pours all his floods;
The doubling storm roars through the woods;
The lightnings flash from pole to pole;

* * *

Near and more near the thunders roll;
When, glimmering through the groaning trees,
Kirk-Alloway seemed in a bleeze!
Through ilka bore the beams were glancing,
And loud resounded mirth and dancing.
Inspiring bold John Barleycorn!
What dangers thou canst make us scorn!
Wi' tippenny we fear nae evil;
Wi' usquebae we'll face the Devil!
The swats sae reamed in Tammie's noddle,
Fair play, he cared na Deils a bodle.
But Maggie stood right sair astonished,
Till, by the heel and hand admonished,
She ventured forward on the light;
And, wow! Tam saw an unco sight!
Warlocks and witches in a dance:
Nae cotillon brent new frae France,
But hornpipes, jigs, strathspeys, and reels
Put life and mettle in their heels.
A winnock-bunker in the east,
There sat auld Nick, in shape o' beast,
A towzie tyke, black, grim, and large,
To gie them music was his charge;
He screwed the pipes and gart them skirl
Till roof an' rafters a' did dirl.
Coffins stood round like open presses,
That shawed the dead in their last dresses;
And by some devilish cantrip sleight,
Each in its cauld hand held a light,
By which heroic Tam was able
To note, upon the haly table,
A murderer's banes, in gibbet airns;
Twa span-lang, wee, unchristened bairns;
A thief, new cutted frae a rape,
Wi' his last gasp his gab did gape;

Five tomahawks, wi' bluid red rusted;
Five scymitars, wi' murder crusted;
A garter, which a babe had strangled;
A knife, a father's throat had mangled,
Whom his ain son o' life bereft,
The gray hairs yet stack to the heft;
Three lawyers' tongues turned inside out,
Wi' lies seamed like a beggar's clout;
And priests' hearts, rotten, black as muck,
Lay stinking, vile, in every neuk:
Wi' mair o' horrible and awfu'
Which even to name wad be unlawfu'.
As Tammie glowered, amazed and curious,
The mirth and fun grew fast and furious;
The piper loud and louder blew;
The dancers quick and quicker flew;
They reeled, they set, they crossed, they cleekit,
Till ilka carlin swat and reekit,
And coost her duddies to the wark,
And linket at it in her sark!
Now Tam, O Tam! had they been queans,
A' plump and strapping in their teens:
Their sarks, instead of creeshie flannen,
Been snaw-white seventeen-hunder linen;
Thir breeks o' mine, my only pair,
That ance were plush, o' guid blue hair,
I wad hae gi'en them off my hurdies
For ae blink o' the bonnie burdies!
But withered beldams, auld and droll,
Rigwoodie hags wad spean a foal,
Lowping an' flinging on a crummock,
I wonder didna turn thy stomach.
But tam kenn'd what was what fu' brawlie.
There was ae winsome wench and walie,
That night inlisted in the core

* * *

(Lang ater kenned on Carrick shore;
For monie a beast to dead she shot.
And perished monie a bonnie boat,
And shook baith meikle corn and bear,
And kept the country-side in fear).
Her cutty-sark o' Paisley harn,
That while a lassie she had worn,
In longitude though sorely scanty,
It was her best, and she was vaunty.
Ah! little kenned thy reverend grannie
That sark she coft for her wee Nannie
Wi' twa pund Scots ('t was a' her riches)
Wad ever graced a dance o' witches!
But here my Muse her wing maun cower,
Sic flights are far beyond her power;
To sing how Nannie lap and flang
(A souple jade she was and strang),
And how Tam stood like ane bewitched,
And thought his very een enriched.
Ev'n Satan glowered, and fidged fu' fain
And hotched and blew wi' might and main;
Till first ae caper, syne anither,
Tam tint his reason a' thegither,
And roars out, "Weel done, Cutty-sark!"
And in an instant a' was dark;
And scarcely had he Maggie rallied,
When out the hellish legion sallied.
As bees bizz out wi' angry fyke,
When plundering herds assail their byke;
As open pussie's mortal foes,
When, pop! she starts before their nose;
As eager runs the market-crowd,
When Catch the thief! resounds aloud;
So Maggie runs, — the witches follow,
Wi' monie an eldritch skreech and hollow.

Ah, Tam! ah, tam! thou'll get thy fairin'!
In hell they'll roast thee like a herrin!
In vain thy Kate awaits thy comin'
Kate soon will be a woefu' woman!
Now, do thy speedy utmost, Meg,
And win the key-stane of the brig;
There at them thou thy tail may toss,
A running stream they dare na cross.
But ere the key-stane she could make,
The fient a tail she had to shake;
For Nannie, far before the rest,
Hard upon noble Maggie prest,
And flew at Tam wi' furious ettle:
But little wist she Maggie's mettle,
Ae spring brought aff her master hale,
But left behind her ain gray tail:
The carlin claught her by the rump,
And left poor Maggie scarce a stump.
Now, wha this tale o' truth shall read,
Ilk man and mother's son take heed;
Whene'er to drink you are inclined,
Or cutty-sarks run in your mind,
Think, ye may buy the joys o'er dear,
Remember Tan O'Shanter's mare.

THE MOCKING FAIRY

WALTER DE LA MARE

"Won't you look out of your window, Mrs. Gill?"
Quoth the Fairy, nidding, nodding in the garden;
"Can't you look out of your window, Mrs. Gill?"
Quoth the Fairy, laughing softly in the garden;
But the air was still, the cherry boughs were still,
And the ivy-tod 'neath the empty sill,
And never from her window looked out Mrs. Gill
On the Fairy shrilly mocking in the garden.
"What have they done with you, you poor Mrs. Gill?"
Quoth the Fairy, brightly glancing in the garden;
"Where have they hidden you, you poor old Mrs. Gill?"
Quoth the Fairy dancing lightly in the garden;
But night's faint veil now wrapped the hill,
Stark 'neath the stars stood the dead-still Mill,
And out of her cold cottage never answered Mrs. Gill
The Fairy mimbling mambling in the garden.

THE NAUGHTY FAY

OLIVER HERFORD

Once a naughty fay
Chanced to sprain her wing;
"At her tricks," they say —
"Naughty little thing!"

Said the little fay
As she lay in pain,
"No more tricks I'll play
When I'm well again."

Time heals everything.
Can this be our fay,
She who sprained her wing
Just the other day?

Can she be this fair
Thrifty little thing,
Sewing up a tear
In a beetle's wing?

Yes, — alas! but oh,
Not a thrifty elf;
Of course she has to sew
What she tore herself!

THE FAIRY CHILD

JOHN ANSTER

༄༅

The summer sun was sinking
With a mild light, calm and mellow;
It shone on my little boy's bonnie cheeks,
And his loose locks of yellow.
The robin was singing sweetly,
And his song was sad and tender;
And my little boy's eyes, while he heard the song,
Smiled with a sweet, soft splendor.
My little boy lay on my bosom
While his soul the song was quaffing;
The joy of his soul had tinged his cheek,
And his heart and his eye were laughing.
I sate alone in my cottage,
The midnight needle plying;
I feared for my child, for the rush's light
In the socket now was dying;
There came a hand to my lonely latch,
Like the wind at midnight moaning;
I knelt to pray, but rose again,
For I heard my little boy groaning.
I crossed my brow and I crossed my breast,
But that night my child departed, —

They left a weakling in his stead,
And I am broken-hearted!
O, it cannot be my own sweet boy,
For his eyes are dim and hollow;
My little boy is gone — is gone,
And his mother soon will follow.
The dirge for the dead will be sung for me,
And the mass be chanted meetly,
And I shall sleep with my little boy,
In the moonlight churchyard sweetly.

DOWN-ADOWN-DERRY

WALTER DE LA MARE

ல~

Down-adown-derry,
Sweet Annie Maroon,
Gathering daisies
In the meadows of Doone,
Hears a shrill piping,
Elflike and free,
Where the waters go brawling
In rills to the sea;
Singing down-adown-derry.

Down-adown-derry,
Sweet Annie Maroon,
Through the green grasses
Peeps softly; and soon
Spies under green willows
A fairy whose song
Like the smallest of bubbles
Floats bobbing along;
Singing down-adown-derry.

Down-adown-derry,
Her cheeks were like wine,
Her eyes in her wee face
Like water-sparks shine,
Her niminy fingers
Her sleek tresses preen,
The which in the combing
She peeps out between;

Singing down-adown-derry.
Down-adown-derry,
Shrill, shrill was her tune: —
"Come to my water-house,
Annie Maroon:
Come in your dimity,
Ribbon on head,
To wear siller seaweed
And coral instead";
Singing down-adown-derry.

"Down-adown-derry,
Lean fish of the sea,
Bring lanthorns for feasting
The gay Faërie;
'Tis sand for the dancing,
A music all sweet
In the water-green gloaming
For thistledown feet";
Singing down-adown-derry.

Down-adown-derry,
Sweet Annie Maroon
Looked large on the fairy
Curled wan as the moon
And all the grey ripples
To the Mill racing by,
With harps and with timbrels
Did ringing reply;
Singing down-adown-derry.
"Down-adown-derry,"
Sang the Fairy of Doone,
Piercing the heart
Of Sweet Annie Maroon;

* * *

And lo! when like roses
The clouds of the sun
Faded at dusk, gone
Was Annie Maroon;
Singing down-adown-derry.

Down-adown-derry,
The daisies are few;
Frost twinkles powdery
In haunts of the dew;
And only the robin
Perched on a thorn,
Can comfort the heart
Of a father forlorn;
Singing down-adown-derry.

Down-adown-derry,
There's snow in the air;
Ice where the lily
Bloomed waxen and fair;
He may call o'er the water,
Cry — cry through the Mill,
But Annie Maroon, alas!
Answer ne'er will;
Singing down-adown-derry.

THE FAIRIES' PASSAGE

JAMES CLARENCE MANGAN

༄

Tap, tap, rap, rap! "Get up, gaffer Ferryman."
"Eh! Who is there?" The clock strikes three.
"Get up, do, gaffer! You are the very man
We have been long, long, longing to see."
The ferryman rises, growling and grumbling,
And goes fum-fumbling, and stumbling, and tumbling
Over the wares on his way to the door.
But he sees no more
Than he saw before,
Till a voice is heard: "O Ferryman, dear!
Here we are waiting, all of us, here.
We are a wee, wee colony, we;
Some two hundred in all, or three.
Ferry us over the River Lee
Ere dawn of day,
And we will pay
The most we may
In our own wee way!"

"Who are you? Whence came you?
What place are you going to?"
"Oh, we have dwelt over-long in this land:
The people get cross, and are growing so knowing, too!
Nothing at all but they now understand.
We are daily vanishing under the thunder
Of some huge engine or iron wonder;
That iron — ah! it has entered our souls."

***

"Your souls? O gholes!
You queer little drolls,
Do you mean — — ?" "Good gaffer, do aid us with speed,
For our time, like our stature, is short indeed!
And a very long way we have to go:
Eight or ten thousand miles or so,
Hither and thither, and to and fro,
With our pots and pans
And little gold cans;
But our light caravans
Run swifter than man's."

"Well, well, you may come," said the ferryman affably;
"Patrick, turn out, and get ready the barge."
Then again to the little folk: "Tho' you seem laughably
Small, I don't mind, if your coppers be large."
Oh, dear! what a rushing, what pushing, what crushing
(The watermen making vain efforts at hushing
The hubbub the while), there followed these words!
What clapping of boards,
What strapping of cords,
What stowing away of children and wives,
And platters, and mugs, and spoons, and knives!
Till all had safely got into the boat,
And the ferryman, clad in his tip-top coat,
And his wee little fairies were safely afloat;
Then ding, ding, ding,
And kling, kling, kling,
How the coppers did ring
In the tin pitcherling!

Off, then, went the boat, at first very pleasantly,
Smoothly, and so forth; but after a while
It swayed and it swagged this and that way, and presently
Chest after chest, and pile after pile

Of the little folk's goods began tossing and rolling,
And pitching like fun, beyond fairy controlling.
　　O Mab! if the hubbub were great before,
　It was now some two or three million times more.
Crash! went the wee crocks and the clocks; and the locks
Of each little wee box were stove in by hard knocks;
And then there were oaths, and prayers, and cries:
"Take care!" — "See there!" — "Oh, dear, my eyes!" —
"I am killed!" — "I am drowned!" — with groans and sighs,
　　　Till to land they drew.
　　　　"Yeo-ho! Pull to!
　　　Tiller-rope, thro' and thro'!"
　　　And all's right anew.

"Now jump upon shore, ye queer little oddities.
　(Eh, what is this? ... Where are they, at all?
Where are they, and where are their tiny commodities?
　Well, as I live!"....) He looks blank as a wall,
Poor ferryman! Round him and round him he gazes,
　　But only gets deeplier lost in the mazes
　　Of utter bewilderment. All, all are gone,
　　　　And he stands alone,
　　　　Like a statue of stone,
In a doldrum of wonder. He turns to steer,
And a tinkling laugh salutes his ear,
With other odd sounds: "Ha, ha, ha, ha!
Fol lol! zidzizzle! quee, quee! bah, bah!
Fizzigigiggidy! pshee! sha, sha!"
"O ye thieves, ye thieves, ye rascally thieves!"
The good man cries. He turns to his pitcher,
And there, alas, to his horror perceives
That the little folk's mode of making him richer
Has been to pay him with withered leaves!

THE FAIRY CHANGELING

DORA SIGERSON SHORTER

Dermod O'Byrne of Omah town
   In his garden strode up and down;
He pulled his beard, and he beat his breast;
And this is his trouble and woe confessed:

"The good-folk came in the night, and they
   Have stolen my bonny wean away;
Have put in his place a changeling,
   A weashy, weakly, wizen thing!

"From the speckled hen nine eggs I stole,
   And lighting a fire of a glowing coal,
I fried the shells, and I spilt the yolk;
But never a word the stranger spoke:

"A bar of metal I heated red
   To frighten the fairy from its bed,
To put in the place of this fretting wean
   My own bright beautiful boy again.

"But my wife had hidden it in her arms,
And cried 'For shame!' on my fairy charms;
She sobs, with the strange child on her breast:

'I love the weak, wee babe the best!'"
To Dermod O'Byrne's, the tale to hear,
The neighbours came from far and near:
Outside his gate, in the long boreen,
They crossed themselves, and said between

Their muttered prayers, "He has no luck!
For sure the woman is fairy-struck,
To leave her child a fairy guest,
And love the weak, wee wean the best!"

THE FAIRY TEMPTER

SAMUEL LOVER

✧

A fair girl was sitting in the greenwood shade,
List'ning to the music the spring birds made,
When sweeter by far than the birds on the tree,
A voice murmur'd near her, "Oh come, love, with me,
In earth or air,
A thing so fair
I have not seen as thee!
Then come love, with me."

"With a star for thy home, in a palace of light,
Thou wilt add a fresh grace to the beauty of night;
Or, if wealth be thy wish, thine are treasures untold,
I will show thee the birthplace of jewels and gold —
And pearly caves,
Beneath the waves,
All these, all these are thine,
If thou wilt be mine."

Thus whisper'd a Fairy to tempt the fair girl,
But vain was his promise of gold and of pearl;
For she said, "Tho' thy gifts to a poor girl were dear
My father, my mother, my sisters are here:
Oh! what would be
Thy gifts to me,
Of earth, and sea, and air,
If my heart were not there?"

from
A MIDSUMMER NIGHT'S DREAM

WILLIAM SHAKESPEARE

Either I mistake your shape and making quite,
Or else you are that shrewd and knavish sprite
Called Robin Goodfellow. Are not you he
That frights the maidens of the villagery,
Skim milk, and sometimes labor in the quern
And bootless make the breathless huswife churn,
And sometime make the drink to bear no barm,
Mislead night wanderers, laughing at their harm?
Those that "Hobgoblin" call you and "sweet Puck,"
You do their work, and they shall have good luck.
      Are not you he?